Antoine Laurain lives in Paris. His award-winning novels have been translated into over twenty languages and have sold more than 150,000 copies in English. *The President's Hat* was a Waterstones Book Club and Indies Introduce selection, and *The Red Notebook* was on the Indie Next list.

Jane Aitken is a publisher and translator from the French.

Emily Boyce is an editor and in-house translator at Gallic Books.

Polly Mackintosh is an editorial assistant and in-house translator at Gallic Books.

'Resist this novel if you can; it's the very quintessence of French romance' *The Times*

'Soaked in Parisian atmosphere, this lovely, clever, funny novel will have you rushing to the Eurostar post-haste ... A gem' *Daily Mail*

'An endearing love story written in beautifully poetic prose. It is an enthralling mystery about chasing the unknown, the nostalgia for what could have been, and most importantly, the persistence of curiosity' *San Francisco Book Review*

Praise for *The President's Hat*:

'A hymn to la vie Parisienne ... enjoy it for its fabulistic narrative, and the way it teeters pleasantly on the edge of Gallic whimsy' *The Guardian*

'Flawless ... a funny, clever, feel-good social satire with the page-turning quality of a great detective novel' Rosie Goldsmith

'A fable of romance and redemption' *The Telegraph*

'Part eccentric romance, part detective story ... this book makes perfect holiday reading' *The Lady*

'Its gentle satirical humor reminded me of Jacques Tati's classic films, and, no, you don't have to know French politics to enjoy this novel' *Library Journal*

The Readers' Room

ANTOINE LAURAIN

The Readers' Room

ANTOINE LAURAIN

Translated by Gallic Books
(Jane Aitken/ Emily Boyce/ Polly Mackintosh)

Gallic Books

London

A Gallic Book

First published in France as *Le Service des manuscrits*
by Flammarion, 2020
Copyright © Flammarion, Paris, 2020

English translation copyright © Gallic Books, 2020
First published in Great Britain in 2020 by
Gallic Books, 59 Ebury Street,
London, SW1W 0NZ

A C IP record for this book is available from the British Library
HB ISBN 9781910477960
PB ISBN 9781910477977

Typeset in Fournier MT Pro by Gallic Books

Printed in the UK by CPI (CR0 4YY)

2 4 6 8 10 9 7 5 3

PART I

Marcel Proust opened his heavy-lidded eyes and gave her a look that was kindly, with a touch of irony, as if to say he knew why she was there. Violaine stared at the author of *In Search of Lost Time* – those dark circles under his eyes, that impeccably combed moustache, the jet-black hair. He was wearing his sealskin coat and sitting on a wooden chair, right beside her bed. His right hand rested on the ivory and silver handle of his cane, while his left smoothly stroked the gleaming pelt of the coat. Violaine turned her head on the pillow and saw that her room was filled with silent, almost immobile visitors. The man in the beige polo neck with wild hair and that strange goatee but no moustache could only be Georges Perec. A black cat perched on a table was enjoying his caresses, showing its appreciation by extending its muzzle towards him. They were looking at each other as if conversing by telepathy.

In cords and a faded denim shirt, Michel Houellebecq stood by the window, gazing into the distance. He was drawing very slowly on a cigarette, wreathed in a cloud of blue smoke. With his stringy hair, long at the back, and his thin lips, he looked like an old witch.

Violaine wanted to call out, 'Michel!' but no sound came from her lips.

She hadn't noticed at first, but there was also a young woman sitting at the foot of her bed, staring at the wall and murmuring things that Violaine could not hear. The woman's hair was loosely knotted, and with her long white dress and profile like a cameo brooch, she was easily recognisable as Virginia Woolf. Violaine closed her eyes then reopened them. They were all still there. She turned towards the other window and there against the light could be seen the tall figure of Patrick Modiano. He appeared to be in urgent conversation with a blonde girl in a black dress, whose face Violaine could not see. He was having to lean over so that he was on the girl's level. The girl nodded.

'Patrick …' Violaine would have liked to say. But once again, not a word passed her lips. However, Modiano did turn slowly towards her and studied her anxiously. He smiled slightly and put a finger to his lips.

'She opened her eyes … She's coming round.' It was a woman's voice.

'Go and get Professor Flavier. Everything's fine, you are not alone,' the voice went on. And Violaine wanted to reply that no, she was definitely not alone. Proust, Houellebecq, Perec, Woolf and Modiano were with her.

Two million French people dream of having their book published if the surveys that have appeared over the years are to be believed. Most of them never get round to actually writing the book. Their draft stays in their head all their lives – a dream that they like to entertain on holiday. Except that they always choose swimming in the pool, or checking the temperature of the barbecue over sitting at a table in the gloom of the house to reread the pages they wrote the day before by the light of their computer screen. They will often talk about the book they have in their head. At first their nearest and dearest are admiring, then, seeing the years pass with nothing produced, they exchange knowing glances every time the would-be author, looking resolute, mentions their upcoming book by saying, 'I'm going to sit down and write it this summer.' But nothing will be written that summer. Nor the next. And certainly not in winter. All those phantom books form a sort of enveloping cloud around literature like the ozone layer around the earth.

Those who will never write more than three pages and an outline are, on the whole, harmless. No readers' room will ever be troubled by their manuscripts arriving in the post. Some other aspiring authors will decide to get down to it properly. Whether it takes them three months or five years of their life, they want to see and to hold in their hands that thick rectangle of white paper, spiral-bound, with, on the cover, a title and their name in Times New Roman size 25 and also the little words 'A Novel'. Their manuscript. This copy, when it has finally been printed out, from the cover page to the very last sentence, will be the fruit of sleepless nights, of rising at dawn, of notes scribbled down in the metro or in airports, of ideas that came to them suddenly in the shower or in the middle of a business lunch like an attacking wasp. The only way to deal with them will have been to write them down as quickly as possible – either jotted down in a red Moleskine, or in Notes on their phone. These sudden ideas will have been crucial for the novel. Or not.

For those people who persevere all the way to 'The End' but know no one in the publishing world, the day will come when they have to send their manuscript out to editors. One morning or evening they will go to a photocopy shop, and ask for ten or twenty copies of their work with a transparent cover, a cardboard back (black or white) and plastic spiral binding (black or white). There are only two colours available. When they get home with their carrier bag as heavy as a little dead donkey, it will be time to slip their covering letter into each copy. Like a letter of recommendation – but from themselves!

Some letters – the kind Violaine prefers – are very simple. Others are unbearably pretentious, claiming for the work a place somewhere between James Joyce and Maurice G. Dantec, or Jim Harrison and Ernest Hemingway. Still others will imply that they know someone influential, without specifying whom – as if that constitutes a veiled threat. The hint of a power that can immediately be invoked in the event that the manuscript is turned down. Violaine kept the funniest, the most ridiculous and the most pathetic in a file in her office for the readers' room archive. The file was labelled 'Insects' which might be taken to mean the file contained information on beetles. But if you knew Violaine, you knew that 'insect' – actually a very ordinary little word – was, when she said it, the ultimate insult.

Phrases such as 'That other insect emailed me this morning …' or directly to someone's face, 'Do you know who you're talking to? Insect …' peppered the speech, usually so refined and friendly, of the elegant forty-something whom everyone found so charming with her green eyes and reddish-brown, shoulder-length hair.

To be called 'Insect' by Violaine Lepage, editor and head of manuscript services, was to be consigned to the lowest form of humanity; it would have been preferable to be a stone. Even authors, journalists, editors, photographers, film producers and agents were not immune from being labelled 'insects'. Once you became an insect, you would be an insect all your life, there was no antidote for that metamorphosis. No return to grace was possible. The status of insect was conferred on you in perpetuity. That was how Violaine operated. She had reigned over her manuscript domain for more than twenty years, having started as a reader before ascending through the hierarchy.

The would-be author was never an insect, nor really a man or a woman. They were not identified by face or age or job. All they were was a name – possibly not even their own – at the top of the first page of their manuscript. What did it matter whether you were called Damien Perron or Nathalie Lefort, Leila Alaoui or Marc Da Silva, whether you were born in 1996 or 1965, if you were a waiter in a brasserie or senior management at AXA, if your family had lived in the Auvergne for ten generations or you were a second-generation immigrant? What mattered was your text; the text you would dispatch one grey morning or one evening from your local post office, where you had been going for ever to send registered letters and formal correspondence, but which that day would take on a special significance. That day you would be more aware of the other people than usual; you would not want them looking over your shoulder and seeing the names of the publishing houses written on the thick brown envelopes along with the words 'For the attention of the manuscript service' like a declaration of helplessness, a sign that you don't have enough influence to get your manuscript read by any other means. The scale will tell you how much postage is needed for the weight and destination of your parcel, all you have to do is press the button for 'No. of parcels'. And the number you enter will be the number of publishers you are entrusting your innards to, your child, the companion of your nights, the torment of your early mornings. Your masterpiece.

Finally, there will be a huge pile which will need both hands to carry out of the post office, and then you will feed the envelopes one by one into the relevant postbox. Usually the destination will be Paris. With two or three exceptions, all the publishers who count have a Parisian address. The dull thud as they land at the bottom of the dark interior of the postbox will perhaps give you the disagreeable sensation that you have just thrown your novel in the bin. Who will care? Who will bother responding? So you will hastily shove the remaining copies into the letterbox as if getting rid of a corpse in the woods at the dead of night.

Once home, you will pour yourself a big glass of wine or whisky. You will feel like crying but you won't, nor will you tell any of your nearest and dearest about your painful postal experience. You won't speak of it, in the same way that you don't tell anyone when you have done something bad for fear that you will be judged, or worse that you will judge yourself as you recount your misdeed.

'Did you send your manuscript off?' someone will ask you that evening.

'Yes,' will be all you say before changing the subject.

'What's your name?'

'Violaine … Lepage.'

'And what do you do?'

'I'm an editor. Where did they go?'

'Who?'

'… Where am I?'

'In hospital, in Paris. Everything's going to be fine. Rest now, I'll come back later.'

Violaine closed her eyes.

'There's no such thing as an undiscovered genius.' Violaine often murmured that phrase like a mantra, as her green eyes scanned first the packages strewn over her desk each morning – the publisher received between ten and fifteen every day – and then the manuscripts piled up on the shelves waiting to be read. Behind each one, a life; behind each one, hope. Every day that a manuscript remains on the shelf is another day of anguish for its author who, every morning, expects to receive a letter in response, or an email or phone call. Their story has captivated the publisher; literature, so long deprived of the author's great talent, will now be properly served.

Five hundred thousand rejections a year, across all publishing houses. What becomes of all those stories? All those fictional characters? The public will never know them, and soon they will be forgotten by the professional readers of publishers' manuscript services. Nothingness awaits them, like those defunct satellites drifting in outer space which even the Deep Space Network no longer monitors. Most authors want their precious manuscript to be returned to them. They can supply a small fortune's worth of stamps so that the publisher will send it back. Or they can go to the publishing house themselves and collect it. Few choose that option. They have dreamed of going to the publisher to be greeted with warm anticipation, to be offered a seat in a large armchair, to say yes, they would like a cup of coffee, to talk a bit about themselves and their book, and finally to produce a beautiful fountain pen and to sign their first contract which they believe – sometimes correctly – will mark the beginning of a new life. So, to go in and ask at reception for the return of their rejected manuscript which an intern would retrieve and hand over with an embarrassed smile and a 'have a good day' would be more than they could bear.

'Madame, I am disappointed that you and your publishing house have not seen fit to take on a manuscript as good as mine. This speaks volumes about the state of our country and its literary culture. It is for that reason that I no longer read French novels and haven't for a long time ...'

'You obviously enjoy turning down the manuscripts of good people and just publish people you know. Editors are scum. Enemies of the people!'

'I have received my manuscript back from you in the post. I placed a hair on page 357 and I see that it is still there. You haven't read my work. I know that publishers never read any submissions.'

Anonymous: 'To the Manuscript Service: you can all go and fuck yourselves!'

'I have decided to end my life. Only the publication of my book could persuade me that life is worth living.'

'I am going to call my friend who is a politician and I think you will see that I'm not just anyone.'

'All my friends and family tell me my book is amazing! You're depriving the world of a wonderful story and your publishing house is missing out on a big success.'

Letters as colourful as those are rare. They form part of a file within the 'Insects' file labelled 'Sometimes they write back!'

The point of a publisher's manuscript service is to find new authors and to publish them. This mission is accomplished two or three times a year. And when it happens, it makes up for all those hours spent reading the prose of strangers, those thousands of opened envelopes, hundreds of reports written, thousands of form letters sent all over the country and sometimes across the world. 'We are sorry to inform you that we will not be publishing your book because despite its many qualities it does not fit our lists.' Yes, two or three times a year the readers' room erupts. A murmured 'I think we have something here' is often the first sign.

That's what happened six months ago with Camille Désencres's *Sugar Flowers*. A text of 170 pages, bound with its transparent cover and cardboard back, sent for the kind attention of the manuscript service. Marie, the youngest of the readers, opened it after she had read the very simple covering letter: 'Hello, my name is Camille Désencres, I hope you will like my book. Best wishes CD.' At page 27 she uttered the words, 'I think we have something here.' Stéphane and Murielle looked up. An hour and a half later Marie had finished *Sugar Flowers*.

'Well?' asked Stéphane.

Marie smiled then uncapped her pen and drew a sun on the cover. 'More like a heatwave, in fact,' she said.

There were three symbols used in the manuscripts department.

Square: reject.

Crescent moon: not uninteresting, worth reworking – or the

author could submit another text which would be considered favourably.

Sun: publish as soon as possible.

The normal procedure on discovering such a gem from the mass of manuscripts was for the reader to rise immediately from their desk, to leave one of the four reading cubicles and walk the ten metres to knock on Violaine's door. But the day *Sugar Flowers* was discovered, Violaine was on a business trip to London.

'Hello Violaine, it's Marie. I think I have found a sun in the manuscripts. Could you let me know how we should proceed since you won't be back for another four days?'

The message remained unanswered for several hours, but then a text arrived, 'Wonderful, Marie. I trust your judgement, but since I won't be able to read it straight away, get Béatrice to read it as soon as possible. Keep me posted.'

'I'll have it taken to Béatrice and let you know.'

Béatrice was the fourth member of the reading room. And, at seventy-five years old, the eldest. Violaine valued her experience and knowledge of contemporary literature. She too had come to the manuscript department via the post, but for once, the envelope had not contained a heavy stack of bound paper, just a simple letter, beautifully phrased and very moving. She explained that she read on average four books a week, and wrote a reader's report for each one, just for fun. Should the publishing house need a manuscript reader, perhaps she could make herself useful.

It would be a great pleasure for her since her days had been free for a very long time. She also said that she lived five minutes away from the publisher. Violaine had contacted her and said she would drop in after a lunch, adding 'I'll make a note of the code for your apartment block and the floor you're on,' only to be told there wasn't one and she should just ring the bell.

There was only one bell with no name. When Violaine rang and announced herself, the heavy door opened onto what appeared to be the principal room of a house. There were Persian carpets, Louis XV armchairs and what looked like a Canaletto on the wall. It might have been a copy, but Violaine did not think so. 'Come up, Madame Lepage, I'm on the first floor!'

Violaine was a little disconcerted by the abrupt change from the outside world to this luxurious interior. She crossed the room which led into another with a tiled floor. And beyond that there was a large sunny garden at the end of which you could make out a flower-covered arbour and a swing seat. Violaine had not known that such an incredible place could exist less than five minutes from the manuscript service. She went up a wide wooden staircase and found herself in an immense drawing room covered in cashmere hangings where the tables and dressers were decorated with fine glass or bronze ornaments. A woman with short white hair and dark glasses sat on a sofa, an incredibly well-toned young man in shorts and T-shirt, his hair tied in a ponytail, by her side. 'Come over … I'm sorry I can't get up, I have trouble walking. It's so kind of you to take the trouble to come here,' said Béatrice.

Violaine shook her hand, noticing the rings, one diamond, one ruby, each the size of a dice, then sat down on one of the armchairs.

Béatrice introduced the young man: 'Marc – I couldn't do without him,' and Marc smiled politely.

As they drank a glass of orange juice and a cup of coffee, Béatrice told Violaine which books she had read recently and others she had read previously. She remembered reading Michel Houellebecq's *Whatever* when it had appeared in 1994 and how she had straight away concluded that he would go far. Marc passed Violaine some reports on novels that had just been published. Béatrice was obviously very good at analysing a text, highlighting the negative and positive aspects.

'I would be very happy to send you over some manuscripts and then we will see if we can work together. And if it works out I will have to give you a salary.'

'I couldn't accept payment,' said Béatrice.

'Yes, you must,' insisted Violaine.

'But, you see ... I own the whole of this street,' murmured Béatrice.

'Excuse me?'

'Yes, there are still some old Parisian families who were able to keep their family's inheritance intact across the generations. This street is not all that big.'

'You mean all the buildings in the street belong to you?'

'Yes, all the residents are my tenants. I have never worked, and that's enabled me to read thousands of books.'

'I'll have to get you to sign a confidentiality agreement. It's a very simple contract by which you would agree not to divulge the contents of the manuscripts,' said Violaine, taking a copy out of her bag and proffering it to Béatrice. Marc immediately took it carefully and signed it himself, leaning on the low table.

'I'm afraid it's not for you to sign, Monsieur ...'

'Marc has power of attorney. Oh, you haven't realised! That's delightful and gives me great pleasure, Madame Lepage.'

'Realised what?'

'I'm blind.'

There was a long silence. 'But ... how do you manage to read?'

'Marc, it's Marc who reads to me. For a good ten years before

24

Marc there was Patrick, and before Patrick, Fabrice ... I have always preferred to have men read to me.'

Before she left, Béatrice asked Violaine if she would do her a favour. Marc had described Violaine from photographs on the internet, but Béatrice asked if she could touch her face. Violaine moved closer and closed her eyes, letting Béatrice's warm, dry hands gently move across her cheeks, forehead and cheekbones. 'You are very beautiful. And you are wearing Guerlain's Eau de Cologne Impériale.'

'I am!' said Violaine, thinking how unique her job was, full of unexpected and mysterious encounters.

'It's your leg that's the problem. Rehabilitation will take a long time and I have to warn you that it's not certain you will ever have full use of it. You will probably have to walk with a stick for the rest of your life.'

'It's not my leg that's the problem, it's this!' said Violaine, tapping the books page in *Le Monde* as it lay open on her bed, and nearly knocking out her drip in the process. Camille Désencres had made it onto the shortlist of the Prix Goncourt ... but had disappeared! No one knew where the author was. 'What are we going to do?' she wailed, addressing Stéphane, Murielle and Marie who were standing by her bed. The three exchanged glances, unsure how to reply, and then turned to Violaine's husband, Édouard, who sighed and said to his wife, 'You've been in hospital for twenty-nine days, eighteen of them in a coma. You have to concentrate on getting better.'

'Your husband is right,' said the doctor, who was disconcerted by this patient who cared more about the selections for literary prizes than about the prospect of limping for the rest of her life.

Marie looked at Violaine fearfully. 'I've emailed again.'

'And?'

'Nothing ... Just like the other times, no answer.'

'Perhaps he's dead ...' offered Stéphane.

'An author doesn't die just before their first book is published, unless they're Stieg Larsson,' Violaine said crisply. The author of the Millennium Trilogy had died suddenly of a heart attack a few months before the publication of the first volume. He never even saw the cover of his first book.

'Even if he – or she – because let's not forget that Camille can be a man or a woman's name – were dead, there would have been a grave, photos of family or holidays, an author biography, but we have none of those. We have nothing!'

'And Bernard Pivot is starting to think we're hiding something,' said Stéphane. 'He warned Pascal he didn't want another author pretending to be someone else, like Émile Ajar.'

'At least everyone knew who he was,' remarked Murielle.

'Right, well, I'll leave you to your literary discussions,' snapped the doctor. 'As I said, you'll be leaving tomorrow at midday. No more editorial boards until you've left. This is a hospital not an office.' And he left.

'Editorial boards are for magazines,' said Violaine. 'Insect …'

With Murielle and Stéphane to his left and Marie on his right, Édouard was pacing up and down the long corridor along with the members of the manuscript department. For a moment he felt like one of those big bosses or government ministers who walk about surrounded by their closest advisers, ready to hang on his every word or agree with his opinions. But Édouard was not talking, he was surreptitiously observing the staff. Stéphane was the most senior member of the department, already there when Édouard had met Violaine fourteen years earlier. Stéphane had hair back then, bright red. In a previous life he had been a secondary school maths teacher. After his divorce he had suffered a nervous breakdown which he referred to as 'going through a bad patch', and this had prompted him to rethink his whole life, starting with his interest in mathematics. Since adolescence he had escaped into books and this seemed to him the only activity that had made him happy throughout those years. He wrote a book on the subject – *Literary Escape* – which the publishing house had published. The book had been an unexpected success: Bernard Pivot had raved about it in his *Journal du Dimanche* column that winter, recommending that a copy should be put under the Christmas tree in every house. And it seemed as if everyone listened. The book was then placed gloriously on the list of books 'recommended by the Department of Education'. It was bought by all the libraries in France, placed on the sixth-form curriculum, and the publishing house, not content with having sold over a million copies, continued to reprint it regularly. When asked if he planned to write another book, Stéphane replied that he had said all he wanted to. He had no more ideas for non-fiction, still less for a novel. So he was offered a position in the readers' room, which had delighted him. Now he was fifty-three years old and part of his income still came from royalties for *Literary Escape* and its thirty-seven translations across the world.

Murielle had previously been a proofreader and the hunt for spelling mistakes and typographical errors had brought her as much joy as gathering mushrooms in September. She tracked them down with a pleasure that bordered on orgasmic and when she came upon a misused past participle or a disjunction between verb and subject, she trembled with happiness. Murielle had worked for large pharmaceutical and automobile companies; she proofread their brochures and financial reports, anything that constituted their communication with the outside world. She had become known to the publisher when she sent them a long letter about the errors she had spotted in two of their recently published books. She was immediately summoned by Charles, then in charge of the publishing house which had been in his family for four generations.

'My father used to tap me on the head with a book when I made a mistake,' he told her.

'Your father should come back and give your authors several taps on the head with a book,' was Murielle's answer.

She was hired there and then. Over the years people noticed that Murielle's comments on page proofs were always spot on: 'This book is going to be a roaring success ...' 'I have no idea who will read this book ...' One day Violaine asked her if she would like to join the readers' room and Murielle's face had lit up.

At twenty-four, Marie was the youngest member of the readers' room. She was still at university and was doggedly writing her thesis on 'The Written Word or the Inert Vectors of Narration'. Marie had decided to identify all the inanimate objects which have played an important part in works of fiction across the last millennium – such as the specimens in Yoko Ogawa's *Ring Finger*, the madeleine in Proust or the little golden key in 'Bluebeard'. She had classified them all by material: fabric, leather, glass, metal, wood ... It was a mammoth task, which, if she came to publish, would run to more than two thousand pages. A literary Himalaya that would take perhaps fifteen more years of her life to complete. Blonde and slim, with pale eyes, Marie was very reserved but her friendly smile more than made up for her lack of vivaciousness. She had started in the readers' room six months previously, having replaced a reader who had reluctantly decided to follow her husband to Beijing.

It was Violaine herself who had brought Marie into the publishing house. Violaine had not used the legendary phrase, 'I think we have something here'; instead she said, 'I've met someone,' which had prompted Stéphane to say in horror, 'You're not leaving Édouard, are you?'

'Of course I'm not leaving Édouard! I mean I've met someone who could perhaps replace Fleur in the manuscript department.'

Violaine omitted to say that she had met Marie at the only Alcoholics Anonymous meeting she had ever gone to. It was her shrink who had recommended she should attend. 'But I'm not an alcoholic!'

'You drink too much.'

'How would you know, you don't live with me.'

'It's you who tells me you drink too much, so you should go and experience a meeting for yourself. You like finding out about things, you'll find it interesting. Even if you don't find it useful and you don't want to continue going, at least you will have taken positive action.'

'You really are a pain, Pierre. Now I feel guilty and I'll have to go.'

That conversation might seem incongruous between a psychoanalyst and their client, but not when the client is also the analyst's editor. Not when that involves the client accompanying them to signings, taking them out to lunch or on holiday with their husband to their house in the Lubéron.

Stéphane, the longest-standing member of the manuscript service, was also the only one who had witnessed Violaine's first meeting with Édouard.

They had met fourteen years earlier at the time of Violaine's meteoric rise at the publishing house. Just after the sudden and unexpected death of Charles, her boss since she had joined the company. One morning Violaine had gone into the readers' room and looked at the metal shelving. 'Those shelves are truly hideous.'

'They really are,' agreed Stéphane.

'And they're so old,' Violaine went on, 'they must have been there since the days of Giscard d'Estaing. We should think about getting new shelves. I'd like you all to put forward some suggestions and I'll set aside a budget.'

The idea of a collegiate decision had not been very successful since they all had a different opinion. The shelves should be made of wood – or glass; straight across – or divided into sections; all the same width – or why not stepped?

'I know a librarian who has stepped bookshelves at home ...'

When Pierre – still a reader at the time – suggested a bookcase in the shape of a tree, with each branch being a shelf, Violaine had to step in. As none of them could agree on which shelves would be best, they would have them made by an interior designer. Édouard

Lavour was chosen, from the design firm Lavour and Sagier. He was the only one in Paris who was willing to turn out to fit an area of only thirty square metres. By return email Édouard declared that he would 'be honoured to enter the famous publishing house which I often pass but which remains a mystery to me'. This had pleased Violaine and she fixed a time for him to come. Stéphane remembered Édouard's arrival as clearly as if it had happened the previous week. He called their meeting 'the staircase encounter'.

Édouard presented himself at reception. Violaine's telephone rang. She emerged from her office calling, 'The designer is here!' The entire manuscript department rose to its feet as one and went to wait at the top of the staircase. Édouard, dark, with short hair, was probably about thirty-five. He gradually slowed down as he neared the top of the stairs; he could not take his eyes off Violaine and seemed mesmerised by the green eyes fixed on him. 'Hello, I'm Violaine Lepage.' She held out her hand and he took it in a daze; he seemed to be transfixed and whispered, 'You're not at all as I imagined.'

Violaine smiled. 'Really? How did you imagine me?'

The designer could not seem to explain and finally just said, 'Not like that.' And in those three words, there was something momentous that Violaine did not pick up. Stéphane, watching their meeting, said to himself that something very special had just occurred, and that he had never seen such a moment accurately described in a novel, perhaps because it was impossible to express in writing. What's more, he had never personally witnessed a man falling head over heels in love with a woman at first sight.

Édouard had spent the entire afternoon producing sketches to represent what he imagined would be the best way to organise the shelves and make use of the space in the readers' room. He devoted himself to the task with the same passion as if he were redesigning the Library of Alexandria. Actually he was spinning the task out while he worked out how to approach Violaine. Stéphane recalled very clearly that there had been a moment when Violaine had come and leant against the door frame just as one of the readers, Solange, had asked the designer whether he was often called upon to build bookshelves in thirty-square-metre offices. Édouard had thought that here was the moment to declare himself, that if he did not, he would regret it his entire life, and that in fact he had no choice. He had looked up at Violaine, then said with what he hoped was his most winning smile, 'When I'm asked by editors as beautiful as Violaine Lepage, yes.' Silence had fallen over the readers' room. Violaine looked at him, her expression unreadable. Édouard knew he had been right to speak out.

As Édouard was thinking about the readers' room and his wife, she was thinking only about Camille Désencres. It was amazing to have been longlisted for the Goncourt prize, but at first Violaine had assumed it was a diversionary tactic – the judges had nominated Désencres just to spite an author or editor who believed their book should be on the list instead. Judges could be capricious – and dangerous. However, since then, Violaine had received more information about why *Sugar Flowers* was unexpectedly on that most sought-after list. Virginie Despentes had assured her that four of the judges, including her, had read the book and found it excellent. It was that simple. What's more, it was good to have a first novel on the list, it made a change from the usual candidates.

'The vampire must have new blood,' thought Violaine on hearing this. That was an expression Charles had often used. From time to time the literary world needs virgin blood in order to regenerate itself. And then a young author will find themselves under the spotlight from their very first book. They then either survive the vampire's bite or wither away for ever, like the two-thirds of authors of first novels who never go on to write a second. Either their next novel is turned down by their editor, or they

33

suffer from writer's block brought on by early success, or by the feeling that they have nothing more to say; there are many ways it can play out. The problem with Camille Désencres was that the vampire may have bitten fiercely, but the prey had vanished, leaving nothing in the spotlight. It was an unusual situation, and had the advantage of piquing the interest of journalists and creating a buzz, but could not last long.

The contact details listed on the cover page of the manuscript had consisted only of an email address: camilledesencres@gmail.com.

Dear Camille Désencres,

The manuscript service and I have read and greatly enjoyed *Sugar Flowers*. We are delighted to inform you that we would like to publish *Sugar Flowers* this coming September. Your novel is highly original both in structure and writing style, and the mystery is exceedingly well drawn. It is rare to find such quality of writing in a first novel.

We would be delighted to welcome you to our list. Please contact me as soon as possible either by replying to this email or by telephoning the manuscript service. We will need your phone number and address and would like to meet you as soon as possible.

Best wishes,
Violaine Lepage
--
Editorial Director
Head of Manuscript Services

Dear Violaine Lepage,

You can't imagine how shocked yet delighted I was to open your email this morning. I can hardly believe it! You really liked my book? I can barely finish this email, I am so overcome.

I'll get back to you as soon as possible.

CD

Dear Camille,

I quite understand your shock and emotion. It might please you to know that out of the three thousand manuscripts we receive each year, we only publish two or three.

But it is now over a week since I heard from you, and I need more details about you, if only to be able to draw up your contract.

Please respond as soon as possible. If you are hesitating because you have a counter-offer, I would urge you not to sign anything before speaking to us.

Violaine Lepage
--
Editorial Director
Head of Manuscript Services

Dear Camille,

I find your silence very worrying. Please respond. We are finalising our autumn schedule and are waiting to hear from you!

Violaine Lepage
--
Editorial Director
Head of Manuscript Services

Dear Violaine,

I'm sorry for taking so long to get back to you. It's not because I am in negotiation with another publisher, it's just that I am away a good deal. Consequently I won't be able to meet you for the next few weeks. Could you have the contract sent to the address below? It's the hotel I stay in when in London. I will return the contract the day I receive it.

Best wishes,
CD

Strathmore Grange Hotel
41 Queen's Gate Gardens
LONDON SW7 5NB
UK

Dear Camille,

We have sent the contract to your address in London and hope that it will arrive soon. I hope you won't think it impolite of me to say that in all my years of publishing I have never come across an author who did not visit their publisher to sign the contract for their first novel.

You are very unusual! And could I ask you who you are? I have reread our emails and realise that I don't even know if you are a man or a woman.

Who is Camille Désencres?

Violaine Lepage
--
Editorial Director
Head of Manuscript Services

Dear Camille Désencres,

We have received the signed contract, thank you for accepting our terms. We are still waiting to hear when we will be able to meet you. We will publish your novel in September and it would be good if you were available for press interviews and photo shoots.

Thank you.

Violaine Lepage
--
Editorial Director
Head of Manuscript Services

I am writing this time from my personal email. Perhaps you will reply to this address.

Camille, please be brave and reveal yourself. I don't know who you are, but you know many things. Who on earth told you about sugar flowers? What else do you know? How are you linked to Normandy?

If your intention is to blackmail me, you are taking an enormous risk, either intentionally or unintentionally.

I am a dangerous woman, don't attack me.

Looking forward to hearing from you.

Violaine Lepage

Violaine,

I wish you no harm.

The book has a life of its own outside my control.
And those who must die will die. All debts will be
repaid.

CD

'Has anyone warned you about Violaine on an aeroplane?' Fleur asked Marie. 'Violaine on an aeroplane,' had sounded to Marie like those books, *Martine at the Beach*, *Martine by the Sea*, *Martine in the Forest*. But Fleur wasn't joking. According to her, Marie, who was going to replace her in the readers' room, would occasionally have to travel with Violaine to book fairs, literary events or to chaperone an author at an important book signing abroad. 'She has a fear of flying.'

'How bad is it?'

'Very bad.'

Before every flight, whether long haul or merely a short hop to Nice, Violaine would read her horoscope and always draw the worst, most dramatic conclusions possible. She would think about all the recent highly publicised accidents which, of course, she had watched avidly on television or the internet, hypnotised like a small rodent before a snake's eyes. The night before she wouldn't sleep. Woken by the alarm early the next morning, she was seized by panic, which Édouard tried to calm by whatever means he could think of since she refused to take any tablets. The panic subsided during the taxi journey but then ramped up on arrival at the departure lounge. The duty-free shops, with their nauseating perfume odours and the takeaway cafés seemed to her like the work of the devil straight out of a nightmare. She would always want to turn tail, to run back to the taxi rank and be taken back home, but instead would disappear into the toilets and gulp down the thirty-five centilitres of Bowmore whisky that she had secreted in her flask out of sight of Édouard the evening before. Then she would chew gum and eventually calm down under the influence of the alcohol. Once on board, she would immediately turn off her air vent, the noise of which drilled into her brain. When she heard the announcements, 'Doors on automatic, cross-check and report,' and 'Cabin crew, please take yours seats for take-off,' she began to tremble imperceptibly and grabbed hold of the armrests, breathing as though she were hooked up to oxygen tanks three hundred metres beneath the sea. When the plane took off, images of Concorde on fire filled her head and she stared fixedly at the lit seat-belt sign, counting each second until it went off, indicating that everything was fine for the moment. She always chose to sit in an aisle seat at the back of the plane so that she could keep looking at the air hostess on the folding seat at the rear. If they looked calm, she was slightly reassured. They became the barometer of her anxiety, and the more they behaved as if everything was normal the less dangerous the flight seemed. As soon as there was any turbulence and the little picture of the fastened seat belt lit up again with a ping, Violaine tensed in her seat and began to pray to practically all the gods in creation that the plane would not pitch, then, with a final jolt, plunge like a stone as the passengers shrieked.

The worst thought was that she had meticulously planned her own death, by buying her tickets, setting her alarm, ordering a taxi and finally settling into her seat on the doomed plane when she should have trusted her instinct and turned back at the door of the airport and run home, or even better, refused to leave her home.

At the first sign of turbulence, her left hand grasped the forearm of her unfortunate travelling companion, her nails digging into the latter's sleeve, sometimes even into her skin, a bit like a cat's claws. For many months, Fleur's arm had retained the bluish marks of a Paris–Frankfurt flight that had run into storms.

These flights left Violaine washed out. She was only able to breathe easily once the plane had landed and was taxiing benignly towards the gate. She had addressed her terror of flying with her shrink, Pierre. He had never accorded it much importance and merely suggested she took a sedative and a good book for the flight.

She was not to know that her worst fears were to be realised on Flight AF 67543.

When the captain announced that they were approaching Paris and about to start their descent, the local time was 6.45 a.m. and the temperature eleven degrees Celsius. Violaine had, of course, not slept a wink nor touched her tray of food. She was watching the peaceful faces of the slumbering passengers, most of them wearing sleep masks. She made sure she kept glancing back at the flip-up seat where the hostess was yawning – a good sign. Marie was fast asleep in the neighbouring seat, her old paperback copy of *Carrie* with turned-down corners and worn spine on her lap. She had carried it around since the age of thirteen when the flyleaf had been inscribed in fountain pen, 'For Marie, all the best for you in this life. Your friend, Stephen King.'

They were on their way back from America. They had had an overnight stop in Bangor in the state of Maine to meet the master of horror in his mythical red and white house surrounded by black iron railings. Famously the gateway was surmounted by delicately wrought bats. Three weeks previously, Violaine had learned via her contacts that Stephen King had just finished a book on imagination. A wonderfully free text, a sort of essay of about a hundred and fifty pages on the cerebral workings of the creative imagination and the effect of this on readers. A brilliant text on the blurred distinction between fiction and reality. According to her sources, few people had read the new book and foreign rights had not yet been negotiated. Violaine had immediately thought, 'I want that book,' and then corrected herself, 'I want us to publish it.' And she had taken out her mobile and scrolled through the list of her contacts until she came to K. She smiled, reflecting that she was surely one of the only French editors to have the personal number of Stephen King.

For this still secret manuscript, Violaine had decided to bypass the usual route taken by literary agents, editors and heads of houses. In doing so she would obviously annoy Fabrice Galland, the director in charge of foreign rights and translations. When he learned that Violaine had negotiated directly with Stephen King, he would no doubt go straight to Pascal, the chairman of the company, and make a complaint. Violaine had decided not to worry about this and had gone ahead and sent a message to the American. A brief text exchange had followed:

- Hello Stephen, I have heard about your new book on imagination. I'm terrified of flying, but I'm coming to see you!
- Good evening Violaine, I love that idea. PS You can call me a bastard for that reply.
- Bastard!

She had gone into the readers' room. 'Marie, would you like to come to the States with me?' Everyone exchanged smiles: now it was Marie's turn for the experience – a sort of aerial initiation to which she had not yet earned the right.

'Let me put it another way,' said Violaine, 'how would you like to come to Maine with me to see Stephen King?'

When Violaine looked out of the window, everything was normal. The memory she would retain of that moment would be as fleeting as a subliminal image: balls of light colliding with the left jet engine. About ten balls in a burst. The impact was deafening and the plane bucked, jolting the passengers awake as thick black smoke belched from the engine. The plane then tipped over to the right and a passenger shouted, 'Fire!' It all happened in a few seconds and the hostess at the back undid her seat belt and hurried up the aisle to the cockpit. Marie opened her eyes and saw Violaine open-mouthed as she stared out of the window. Then she in turn saw the engine wreathed in smoke. The right wing was hit by a second impact and the plane plunged into an air pocket that compressed their hearts like crumpled paper. Oxygen masks dropped down from above and dangled on their clear tubes like novelty toys from a joke box, as the cabin vibrated as if the plane was about to explode.

'Birds have flown into our engines!' cried the hostess. 'Put on your oxygen masks!' She repeated this in French, as Violaine began to tremble, incapable of raising her arm to take her mask. She felt as though the previous seconds had drained her body of blood, and she was now sure that she would never see Édouard or her apartment or the readers' room ever again. Her worst nightmare had come true; she was going to die in a plane crash. And she would cause Marie to die as well. In a few minutes it would all be over. The businessman to her right across the aisle had his head in his hands, sobbing nervously. The plane swung about like a leaf in the wind and there was nothing but shouting.

'We're not going to die,' murmured Marie.

'We are!'

'I can't die, not right now,' Marie assured her. 'So you won't die either.'

Violaine could no longer hear her; the pressure had blocked her ears and she felt she was experiencing the first symptoms of a heart attack. The last thing she was aware of in that moment was Marie's perfume: the smell of jasmine floated in the air.

That's what would she would retain from her time on earth. Marie's perfume. The smell of jasmine.

'Brace position!' ordered the pilot, as the metallic thud of the wheels unfolding was felt beneath their seats. The seconds that followed were confusing for Violaine and Marie. They thought they were still in the air but actually the plane was a few metres off the ground. It was only from images on television that they learned what had happened after the event. The pilot, with only one working engine, had chosen to land by gliding down to the runway, attempting with the power that remained to reduce the impact of the landing as much as possible. The landing gear was crushed instantly and the plane went into a skid that the fuselage could not withstand: it split in two between the side doors and the floor gave way in the middle, taking ten aisle passengers with it, one of whom was Violaine. That evening, the images shown on a loop on French news and picked up by channels across the world depicted the plane broken into two sections on the runway at Roissy, surrounded by emergency vehicles, the tarmac covered in foam from the fire engines, and teams freeing the wounded with the help of electric saws. It was a miracle that no one died. Ten people were injured, five of them, including Violaine, seriously. Marie escaped unhurt. All the commentators and experts were united in their praise for the pilot's handling of the incident and agreed that it had been a freak accident: first the left engine had literally swallowed a formation of fifteen wild geese, then a minute later the same had happened on the right.

Violaine had not seen a corridor of light, nor any angels. There had been no bliss or parade of departed loved ones. Nothing.

Dear Violaine,

Wherever you are, rest assured that I heard about the plane, your injuries and your coma. I know all about accidents, hospitals and suffering. I am very sorry to have been in a way responsible for what happened to you. The least I can do is give you and your publishing house the French rights to my book on the power of the imagination. My agent will see to that.

Wake up … now!

Your friend,
Stephen King

While she was still in a coma, Violaine had had to be operated on twice, despite the risk, to avoid amputation of her leg. A scar, three centimetres wide, now meandered from the top of her thigh down to her heel. She also had several flesh wounds, as if meteorites had exploded, leaving star-shaped holes. A complicated system of fine brushed-steel tubes and bolts encased her calf and from above her knee to mid-thigh. When she first saw them she had been reminded of David Cronenberg's film *Crash* in which Rosanna Arquette, at the height of her beauty, had to have steel braces on both legs, following a car accident – which had an expectedly erotic effect on men which she fully exploited.

When Violaine returned home, supported by Édouard and walking awkwardly with her crutch, she had sat down on the sofa and he sat in the armchair facing her. She closed her eyes, then opened them again on the familiar decor, before looking at her husband. 'I thought I would never see this place again.' And Édouard had concurred, saying, 'I thought I would never see you again. But here we are.' He went over to sit beside her and take her in his arms. Violaine rested her head on his shoulder. 'What would I do without you?' Édouard could find nothing to say in response, merely stroking her cheek then resting his on her hair. And they stayed like that for a long while in the afternoon light, without saying a word.

Taking a shower proved to be a complicated exercise. She had to lay her crutch along the wall of the Italian shower, make sure that the gel recommended by the doctor ran over her leg and rinse the stainless-steel brace with the showerhead, all without slipping. Édouard stayed beside her, ready to catch her if she lost her balance. Then the leg had to be dried with the hairdryer – it was impossible to get a towel between the steel rods. The scars had to be sprayed with antiseptic and finally she had to give herself an injection of powerful painkiller using a disposable syringe. 'Just stick the needle into your calf and press the plunger.' Easier said than done.

Violaine asked Édouard to leave her alone in the bathroom. He wandered into the sitting room and stood in front of 'their' wall. They had each appropriated a part of the wall to pin up photographs that were precious to them. Édouard's were of interiors he had created; some of the pictures showed him in the background with members of his team and his partner, Marc Sagier. There were also framed interior decorating magazine covers celebrating his creations. Violaine's photos were all of her. Violaine in dark glasses with Haruki Murakami; Violaine with John Irving, pointing to the author's tattoo; Violaine with Philippe Sollers – she had stolen his cigarette holder; Violaine with Houellebecq, both smoking, their cigarettes held between third and fourth fingers; with Philip Roth – she had her arm round him on a bench in Central Park; with Modiano – they were both looking up at the sky; Violaine with Stephen King, he with his hand out, preventing her from speaking; finally, a curiosity, Violaine with the Rolling Stones – she was sticking her tongue out.

While Édouard was lost in memories in front of the wall of photos, Violaine was looking at herself in the full-length bathroom mirror. Naked, with her left leg in its contraption, she was regarding herself in horror. She moved closer to the mirror and saw circles under her eyes and wrinkles that had not been there a few weeks earlier. She also noticed her hair, now too long, was losing its red tint. She stepped back. 'I've lost at least twelve kilos,' she murmured before picking up a hairbrush and using it to measure the distance from the bottom of her breasts to her belly button. The distance was no longer the same and Violaine flung the brush against the wall. She turned to look at her hips in the mirror and the braced leg with the scar running down her flesh. And then she closed her eyes.

A heart-rending sound like the cry of a she-wolf rang out. Their neighbours had recently acquired a white Japanese dog that resembled a bear and sometimes, in the afternoon, it would start to howl for no apparent reason. Édouard was thinking it was painful to listen to, when he realised that the sound was not coming from below, it was there in the apartment. He ran to the bathroom. 'Violaine?' he shouted, opening the door without waiting for a reply.

Violaine was crouching in front of the mirror and her distressed cries were reaching a fever pitch.

'I know it's all too much to bear at the moment, darling. But I'm here. I'm here ...'

'Don't look at me! Go away!' she shouted, struggling as he tried to take her in his arms. 'I don't want anyone to see me! Get out!'

'It's all right,' said Édouard. He tried to hold her as she pushed him away violently, then relaxed against him.

'It's your fault!' she cried, hitting the floor with her hand.

'Yes, it is my fault,' agreed Édouard, ready to do anything to calm her.

'You let me take off in that plane!' she sobbed. 'You shouldn't have done that!'

'No, no, I shouldn't,' he said, stroking her hair. 'I'll never let you go away again.'

'Never again!' echoed Violaine. 'You must never let me go away, never ...' She was out of breath now. 'You're never to let me go away ...'

The very next day, Violaine returned to work. As she entered her office, her heart lifted at once again seeing the waxed parquet, the red Garouste and Bonetti rug and her black leather swivel chair on wheels. The light was coming in through the large window framed by the yellow curtains chosen to create an illusion of sun – an antidote to the often grey Parisian sky. Her table was there with its jumble of manuscripts, Post-it notes, loose papers, reviews, printed emails with underlinings, pens and rubber-tipped pencils, and above it, pinned to the wall, assorted notes. There was method in her madness, she was fond of saying. And the fact was that she could always find, between a packet of sweets and a ball of paper, the very sheet of paper she needed with the terms of a contract to be negotiated, or the brilliant ideas jotted down during a lunch with an author.

There was a lingering smell in the air of coal, hot and dry, an odour like rancid hay. The instantly recognisable smell of cigarettes. Violaine was outraged. 'Who's been smoking in here?' The assembled members of the readers' room looked at each other in much the same way as they had at the hospital. Pascal, the chairman and managing director of publishing, who had helped Violaine up the stairs with her crutch, remained impassive, sporting the vague smile that he wore in all circumstances. Then he turned to her and, in an attempt at humour, said, 'I agree, it's absolutely shocking!' But Violaine did not see the funny side, especially as smoking had been banned in offices and public spaces since 2008.

'No one has been smoking in your office,' Marie assured Violaine.

'Yes, they have – it stinks of cigarettes.'

'It's the smell of your cigarettes, from before,' said Stéphane. 'We emptied the ashtrays and put your lighters here.'

'And your last packet is on the table,' added Marie.

'Thank you,' murmured Violaine. 'Thank you …' And she went towards her desk.

'We'll leave you to settle in,' said Pascal, and everyone returned to their own work.

She closed the door and looked at the lighters: a Dunhill, two Duponts and a Cartier. All steel, or gold. She had a vague feeling of déjà-vu but it was only fleeting, like those names you have on the tip of your tongue but which elude you. She opened one to light it. The steel Dupont cap pinged as it flipped back. A little blue and yellow flame. She closed it with the characteristic click. A sound she had heard before, but nothing more. She picked up a packet of cigarettes – Benson & Hedges Gold 100s – breathed in the honey odour of the white sticks, put one in her mouth and chose the gold Dunhill. The tip of the cigarette glowed. Violaine took a puff, filling the room with a milky blue cloud. Immediately, the image of Michel Houellebecq, smoking by her hospital window, came to mind. It was so vivid that she turned to see whether Proust was sitting in the chair, or Perec was stroking a cat, or Virginia Woolf was talking to herself, or Modiano was murmuring in the ear of a mysterious young blonde woman. No, no one was there. The smell of tobacco which had passed from her throat to her nostrils was unpleasant and definitely 'new'. She took a second drag and swallowed the smoke. She choked and bent over coughing so violently that Magali, the secretary, knocked on the door to make sure everything was all right. Her eyes red and streaming, Violaine opened the door and managed to ask for a glass of water.

Now the glass was empty and Violaine, in her chair, stared fixedly at her mobile. Eventually she picked it up and rang her psychiatrist, Dr Pierre Stein. When his assistant told her he was in a consultation, Violaine declined to leave a message, saying she would call back. She immediately rang his mobile and he picked up straight away. She could hear conversation in the background and the hiss of a coffee machine.

'Pierre?'

'Violaine.'

'Am I disturbing you?'

'No, I'm in the café.'

'Pierre … apparently I smoke.'

'Same here, apparently I smoke – a packet a day for the last forty years; tell me something I don't know. Tell me about you. How are you?'

'I am telling you about me, Pierre. I have no recollection of ever having smoked.'

'Seriously?'

'Yes.'

'Is anything else worrying you?' He sounded suddenly sharp, almost disagreeable.

'Yes …'

Now all she could hear were the sounds of the café in the background and then, 'Come and see me this evening.'

'Cigarettes, clothes, jewellery,' wrote Violaine. After her meltdown in the bathroom, she had opened her wardrobe to get out her grey skirt and red and black top. She was very surprised to find an orange silk dress, and also a blue patterned one. She went through all the hangers one by one, recalling where she had bought the clothes. That purple dress with the belt had been bought with Édouard in Rome, those off-white trousers came from London, the pale-grey coat with the black collar from San Francisco and the beige strappy top from the swap shop in the twentieth arrondissement. Her wardrobe was like a visual record of all the trips and journeys she had made around the world.

Now the orange silk dress and the blue patterned one lay on the sofa, along with a good twenty others, limp on their hangers. Violaine stared at the heap. It looked as though twenty women had sat down on the sofa one by one, then suddenly evaporated, leaving their clothes behind. She had no memory of these twenty outfits. No memory of ever having worn them. No memory of any boutique in France or elsewhere she could have bought them. Although she was distressed and not a little panicked, there was also an amusing side to this: as if a mischievous devil or a Father Christmas had come and hung in her wardrobe clothes of exactly her size and taste. When she opened her jewellery box, it was just the same: some of the rings and necklaces were utterly familiar, but others she didn't recognise. The same hand that had added mystery dresses to her wardrobe had put a handful of jewellery in her jewellery box. She had never seen the coral earrings before, or the gold and pearl ring, and certainly not the sapphire mounted in the silver ring.

'Édouard?'

'Would you like my help with getting dressed?' he said, opening the door.

Violaine pulled the orange dress from the bottom of the pile and held it up in front of her. 'Have you ever seen me wearing this dress?'

'Dozens of times, why?'

'Nothing.'

The incident happened a long time ago. But this winter afternoon, in the city, on the terrace of this café under this lunar-grey sky, I have made my decision: all debts will soon be repaid.

It is time to tell the world about the honest people who lived peaceably in that village in the French countryside and also a little, not too much, about those others, the others who stole their lives. I am the angel of death and I have returned just to tell the story. Listen to me.

That was the opening of *Sugar Flowers*.

camilledesencres@gmail.com

Violaine,

I wish you no harm.

The book has a life of its own outside my control. And those who must die will die. All debts will be repaid.

CD

The latest email from the author was open on Violaine's screen. She clicked to the sales figures tab to check *Sugar Flowers'* position in the bestseller list. It had moved up from eighteenth place to fifteenth. They had already reprinted three times. Press coverage was continuing. But nothing could be done for radio or television without Camille Désencres. François Busnel had invited Camille onto *La Grande Librairie* but it had had to be explained that while the author was very flattered, they did not wish to appear on television at the moment. The line taken by the publishing house was as follows: the author was very private and did not want any exposure; no, it wasn't someone working for the publisher using a pseudonym; yes, the author would shortly make themselves known. To the question: 'Is it a man or a woman?' the answer was always, 'You'll soon see.'

Violaine took out Béatrice's reader's report.

> *Sugar Flowers*: On the death of her parents, a young woman learns that the people she thought were her parents were actually her grandparents. Her real mother had fled after her birth. She was the product of a gang rape. She sets out to find her mother and kill the four men who raped her one by one.
>
> The reader does not know whether the narrator of the story is the young woman herself or a witness to the events, either man or woman. The book is like a long confession. The crimes, all committed with an old pistol dating back to the war, have a dreamlike quality, which might indicate that they are a fantasy. The book is not a thriller, even though it draws on the same structures. The prose style is almost hymn-like. I

would almost say the entire novel is a plea to fate to correct past wrongs.

It is one of the most singular texts I have ever read. It is deeply moving and I can't stop thinking about it. I am also giving it a sun and so I support Marie, who was the first reader. Talking of whom, I still haven't met her; perhaps she could come and see me one day.

P.S. The title is very good. It refers to the sugar sculptures that artisan patissiers sometimes make.

'Violaine?' called Magali, knocking on the half-open door. 'Reception says there's a girl, looks a bit like a punk, who sent you a manuscript about fortune tellers after hearing you talk about fate on France Culture. She really wants to see you.'

'Yes, I have it here,' said Violaine, indicating a manuscript about a hundred pages long, on paper that looked more like parchment than the standard white paper, spiral-bound in black or white, which usually arrived in the manuscript department. This one was sewn with hemp, not bound. Violaine had received this curiosity just before her plane accident. The text was handwritten in Chinese ink, and followed the forgotten history of tarot cards and the once famous fortune tellers, whom no one has heard of nowadays. The author, Karine Visali, had drawn the tarot cards with pen and inks of various colours, and annotated the drawings with interpretations of the cards' meanings. She must have spent months on this single copy – which was completely irrelevant to a manuscript department seeking new novels.

'She's probably come to collect her manuscript. I'll take it down to her.' Magali took the manuscript from the pile and left.

Violaine, who had said nothing, picked up her phone and called reception. 'Violaine here. Magali is on her way down with a book of magic spells to give to the punk. Ask them all to come up to my office. Yes ... all three: Magali, the spell book and the punk. Thank you.'

'That represents death?' asked Violaine, pointing to a card depicting a skeleton in a red habit.

'Yes, but it's death avoided. It's your accident, I think.'

For ten minutes the cards had been laid out in a long line on the low table where Violaine took coffee with her authors. Some had been turned face up, but not all of them. 'Punk' had been an unfair description of Karine Visali. Certainly, her hair was shaved on the left side of her head and the rest fell in a curtain she had decorated with coloured beads, but she definitely did not have a Mohican, or safety pins, or a studded leather jacket. She was wearing faded denim dungarees, stone bangles and feathered earrings. Violaine, watching as Karine's fingers with their bitten nails moved over the line of cards, counting as she went, decided she could not be more than thirty. Four, five ... she turned over a card showing a man in eighteenth-century costume lying on a daybed holding a flaming candelabra.

'The adviser; he is master of your dreams and secrets. He helps you. You have a confidant or ... shrink?'

Violaine looked at her in silence. Then she merely murmured, 'Go on.'

'One, two, three,' Karine continued, and turned over two more cards. On each of the cards you could see a meeting in a sort of reception room in a castle; one card showed only women, the other, only men. 'Many people are talking about you. You are the focus of attention.' She turned over a new card, revealing a man carrying a bundle of clothes over his shoulder. 'The traveller.' Karine then counted eight cards and put her finger on the one with the sphinx and the hourglass. 'Someone made a very long journey to come and see you.' She then turned over a card representing a dragon in front of a chest filled with gold pieces. 'The secret,' she murmured, 'the traveller bears a secret. Choose one of the cards that are face down.' Violaine touched one and Karine moved it gently away from the line of cards. 'Now two more, please,' and Violaine indicated two others which Karine also moved away.

She turned over the first one – the leper – and then the other two simultaneously – the prisoner, the queen.

'This is very strange, there is a problem with identity,' said Karine as she put her finger on the traveller card. 'The traveller has no identity; everything revolves around the queen. You are the queen; there is a problem to do with the past and memory. Five, six, seven ...' She turned over a card showing a barking dog. 'Vengeance. Eight, nine ... Death, and three, the meeting of men. The traveller bears a secret that threatens the men, and this secret brings revenge, but it spares the queen. It's as if some elements have been forgotten. Do you know someone who has a problem with their memory?'

Violaine stared at her again, before announcing, 'We will publish your book. In our coffee-table books collection. We'll reproduce your hand-drawn illustrations; it will be very beautiful. Please go on.'

'You're joking! You're really going to publish my book?' Karine's eyes were shining with tears.

'Keep going, stay focused.'

'Take the cards without looking at them and cover all the cards in the line.'

Violaine laid a card on top of each one in the line of thirteen. Karine turned them over, placing them on top of the first cards, creating a second line, and Violaine saw that the king had appeared on top of the queen.

'Have you a partner, or a husband?'

'Yes.'

'That's him.'

'That happened by chance ...' said Violaine softly.

'There is no chance in this game. Three, four, five, the alchemist, six, seven, the librarian. Nine ... the queen. Do you have a problem with a book?' Violaine closed her eyes and could not think of a reply.

'Twelve, thirteen,' continued Karine, stopping on a man in a suit, his arms crossed: the provost.

'The provost?'

'That's an old name for a policeman or lawyer. Eight, nine ... the road, eleven, twelve, the secret, thirteen, the queen. The provost is on the way, but the king and queen triumph. However, I don't know what that is.' Karine pointed to two cards: the meeting of men and death. 'It's as if some must die. As if that has been written.'

'Thank you, Karine,' whispered Violaine, 'we'll draw up your contract.'

Once the fortune teller had left, Violaine picked up the packet of cigarettes, looked at it and hurled it into the bin. She tidied the lighters away in a drawer and left her office to go into the readers' room, leaning on her crutch.

'Are you all right?' asked Murielle.

'Yes, are you?' replied Violaine, smiling.

'Only squares at the moment,' sighed Stéphane, 'not even a crescent moon in sight.'

'And as for suns …' added Marie, looking despairing.

'You can't complain, you found the last one!' retorted Murielle. And Violaine smiled again, watching them talk to each other without taking their eyes off their manuscripts. This really was where her life was, between these walls, in this room, where she had started out. She had fought so hard to attain all this. Her success had been a miracle, she thought as her eye fell on Édouard's bookcases. Yes, her entire life was linked to this room.

'Violaine?' called Magali. 'Reception rang, there's someone from the police to see you.'

Pierre Stein's waiting room, like his consulting room, reflected his personality: refined and vaguely unsettling. Stein had chosen red fabric for the walls, deep carpets, silk cushions and antique lamps positioned in the room to create a subdued light. Red was, according to him, a stimulating colour, and it was good if patients arrived on his couch fully awake. His consulting room was much larger than the waiting room and the light slightly dimmer. The walls were lined with subtly lit bookshelves which held rows of books or ornaments. He did have some recent titles, but most of his books dated back centuries and had informed his knowledge of 'pre-psychoanalysis': studies from the eighteenth century of hysteria or nymphomania, works from the nineteenth century on various psychiatric disturbances ranging from lycanthropy to Capgras delusion, in which patients believe that a close relative has been replaced by an impostor. The shelf of which he was most proud held about a hundred works on murder and the psychiatric study of crime. If his literary tastes could be considered worrying, his collection of ornaments was much more wholesome, consisting of folk art pottery. Earthenware jars, jugs and plates, all in the naïve style, filled the ornamental shelves. You could make out images of animals frolicking in bucolic settings; farmers, priests and even road menders featured. Stein found his collection reassuring, and criticised analysts who displayed African masks, or voodoo statues in their consulting rooms.

There were never any magazines in the waiting room. Only a few books. *In Search of Lost Time*, the Pléiade edition, lay nonchalantly on the low table, alongside Tolstoy and a collection of short stories by Maupassant. Violaine sat on the sofa, absently stroking one of the polished steel rods of her leg brace as she recalled her meeting with Detective Inspector Tanche.

Sophie Tanche had been medium height, slightly overweight, with short brown hair. Probably well into her thirties, Violaine decided. She had been wearing a black leather biker jacket, obviously pretty old. It was shiny in places and looked too small, as if Sophie had kept the garment for sentimental reasons even though it no longer really fitted her.

'Detective Inspector Sophie Tanche, Rouen regional crime squad,' had been how she introduced herself.

'It's cool here,' she observed, looking about her.

'Yes, it's all right.'

'They're beautiful, those yellow curtains.'

'They're silk, from Lyon; my husband is an interior designer.'

'Handy to have a husband who's an interior designer,' Sophie Tanche had said, and Violaine had felt that she was voicing out loud something deeply personal.

Violaine had offered coffee that Sophie declined, saying she drank far too much of it. She accepted sparkling water instead, so Violaine rose and limped over to the cupboard with the fridge containing bottles of water, soda and whisky.

'Are you injured?'

Violaine turned to her and lifted her long skirt as far as her hip, revealing the contraption on her leg.

The inspector whistled. 'Car accident?'

'Plane. I was in the Roissy plane crash.'

'Oh! The huge plane that split in two?'

The desire to pour a glass of Bowmore and down it in front of the police officer was strong, but she contented herself with sighing deeply. She poured two glasses of water. The policewoman gulped hers straight down. Violaine did not touch hers; she was watching Sophie. She tried to analyse her the way she did the first time she met an author. Modest and friendly or pretentious and unbearable? Would it be easy to get on with them in the months and perhaps years they would work together? Intelligent? Where were they from? What was their background? Did they sometimes lie? Were they shy or did they pretend to be? Were they trustworthy? Would they write another book?

Violaine's first impression of Inspector Tanche led her to think the following: she was trying too hard to be pleasant, but was probably just shy; she was socially awkward; had fought hard to get where she was; was much more intelligent than she was willing to let on; she was deeply unhappy.

'You have the most amazing green eyes; people must tell you that all the time.'

'True.'

There was a silence in which they could hear the bubbles fizzing in the water.

'Right,' said the inspector, 'we've talked about silk, the colour of your eyes, the plane crash; now I'm going to tell you why I'm here.'

She reached down into her satchel and took out a copy of *Sugar Flowers*. 'You recognise this book of course?'

'Yes, I published it.'

'And I've read it. Do you smoke?'

'No.'

'Yet it smells of cigarettes in here.'

'It's fine for you to smoke, Inspector.'

'Ah, thank you,' and Sophie took out a packet of Marlboro Reds and a Bic lighter. When she spoke again, it was through a cloud of smoke.

'In the book that you published, four murders are described. The first' – she paused – 'bears a striking similarity to a case I investigated last year.'

'I can't see any link between a novel and a police case,' ventured Violaine.

'Well, I can.' Sophie opened *Sugar Flowers* to a page she had marked with a Post-it and read aloud:

> 'As the first iridescent purple rays of the sun finally break through the fog, they will be there. At prayer, the bodies already stiff, like clay statues, they will both be there in the clearing. My first will be kneeling contemplating his sins. With a bullet straight to the forehead, his spirit will have returned to the devil – only he will have use of him for the centuries to come. My second will be looking at the sky without finding any hope of redemption. The Luger P08, whose bullets are stamped with the double 's' of the Waffen SS, had proved to be the perfect instrument for this mission. The weapon of bastards to kill bastards, the weapon of scum to kill scum. The ignoble weapon was given to me to follow the path of light.'

'Beautiful passage,' commented Violaine.

'Yes,' agreed Sophie, as she reached into her bag again and took out a file from which she extracted a colour photo. 'And here is a very beautiful illustration.' She placed the photo on the low table in front of Violaine. The picture was of a dark-haired man of about fifty, in a tracksuit, kneeling amongst dead leaves, his head bent forward, a dark hole between his eyes. At his side, a blond man of the same age, also in sportswear, in the same position. But his head was thrown back, his eyes bulged, his mouth was wide open and he appeared to be looking at the sky in horror. There was a dark hole between his eyes.

'The first is a man called Sébastien Balard. He owns a nightclub in Normandy near Rouen, called Thor. He inherited it from his father. The second is Damien Perchaude, the notary in a village called Bourqueville. They had known each other since school and went running together every Sunday morning. This time they did not make it back. That was a year ago. Interviews with their nearest and dearest, forensics, recreating their movements – I've moved heaven and earth to solve this.'

Violaine looked at the photo but her eye was drawn to Sophie's hands. She was massaging her ring finger to discreetly remove a gold cabochon ring with green stones. She put it on the table by her glass; the ring had left a mark on her finger.

'Sébastien Balard was dealing drugs at his nightclub, coke and ecstasy. Let's just say he had dealings with some very dodgy people. The club had been closed down three times, but he always managed to get it opened again. His mate Perchaude had shares in the club. At the moment the theory is that this was a settling of scores between drug dealers. It's the only lead we have. Are you listening to me, Madame Lepage?'

Violaine was hypnotised by the inspector's ring and found it hard to look up. 'Yes, I'm listening, Inspector. You said it's the only lead you have.'

'Yes,' continued Sophie Tanche, 'we don't have much to go on. Some minor and not so minor criminals were arrested. All have been released. One of the Romanian drug barons who control several networks in Normandy was also arrested. But we found no threatening messages, no suspicious calls from his mobile. No DNA found at the crime scene. The investigation had stalled. And then your book appears ... and throws a radically different light on the affair.'

As Violaine said nothing, the inspector simply continued. 'In fact, there were four friends: Sébastien Balard, dead, Damien Perchaude, dead, and two others: Marc Fournier, one of the sons of the ex-mayor of Bourqueville, who became a taxi driver, and Pierre Lacaze, a head chef who left ten years ago to open a French restaurant in Los Angeles but who has just returned to France. Since August he has been in Paris at the restaurant Le Louis XIX.' She drew on her cigarette and flicked the ash into a small dish. 'If I follow the thread of the novel that you have published, two other men must still die: the taxi driver and the head chef.'

The inspector paused. 'And there's something else.'

'What else, Inspector?' Violaine's eyes moved from the photo to the ring.

'Balard and Perchaude were killed with a Luger P08 with bullets stamped with the double 's' of the SS. But this detail was never disclosed in the press. I'm going to have to ask you to give me the contact details for your author, Camille Désencres.'

'I'm happy to see you,' declared Pierre Stein, taking Violaine in his arms. Pierre, with his grey-white hair and carefully maintained three-day beard, was looking more and more like Serge Gainsbourg. What had been just a passing impression a few years ago was now an uncanny likeness, especially in the darkness of his office. Violaine lay down on the couch covered in the statement red cashmere, and Pierre produced a bottle of champagne and two flutes.

'From my cellar,' he announced. 'Let's drink to your return to the land of the living. Champagne Salon 2007,' and he popped the cork and filled the two glasses which they clinked before he sat back down in his chair.

They each sipped the precious bubbling liquid.

'Very good,' said Violaine.

'It ought to be, since it's a Salon 2007,' remarked Pierre wryly, 'at five hundred euros a bottle!'

'Don't be vulgar, Pierre, please. I'm only drinking the royalties I've paid you,' retorted Violaine.

Pierre smiled and let a silence fall.

He drew his standing ashtray nearer to him and lit a cigarette. Smoke swirled around him like steam.

'I didn't know I smoked, and I don't miss it at all.'

'How lucky you are.'

'I'm serious. And there's another thing, I don't recognise a quarter of my clothes and jewellery.'

Pierre drank from his flute. 'For example?'

'An orange dress, very elegant. I don't remember buying it but Édouard has seen me wear it several times.'

Pierre opened his computer. 'Go on.'

'The jewellery ... I have no recollection of some of the rings and earrings. None at all. It's as if they were put there by someone else. I'm frightened, Pierre. I'm frightened I have forgotten other things.'

'Have you had a brain scan?'

'All normal, apparently.'

'The orange dress. Is it Bottega Veneta?'

'Yes, how did you know?' said Violaine, sitting up on the couch.

'No memory of clothes or jewellery? Or cigarettes, even though you smoked more than a packet a day ... That's fascinating,' he said with a smile.

'What's fascinating about it?'

'The brain, Violaine, the labyrinth of the brain ... is fascinating,' he murmured, playing elegantly with the cigarette between his fingers. Then he set it down in a glass ashtray and the smoke rose in a straight line up towards the ceiling. He opened a drawer in his desk then went back to his chair beside the couch. 'And do you remember these?' he asked, putting into her hand a collection of gold and silver rings, most of them decorated with precious stones.

Violaine looked at them glittering in the palm of her hand. 'What is this?' She sounded a little afraid.

'You don't know what this is about?'

'No, where did you get these rings?'

Pierre smiled again. 'Fascinating,' he repeated before rising and draining his champagne standing in the middle of the room.

'Violaine, you are a kleptomaniac. You have been bringing me jewellery for years. I have a whole collection in my desk drawer. You steal all the time. You steal dresses as well, and you tell me about it in our sessions; you describe them in great detail. I have notes on all of them. Twice I have had to collect you from the police, when you stole from Cartier and from Dunhill. I have written dozens of letter so that you would not be charged. Your biggest fear is that Édouard might find out. And even so … you have no memory of all this.'

'You're lying!' protested Violaine.

'Absolutely not!' replied Pierre Stein, stung. He went over and removed the drawer and placed it on Violaine's knees. Inside were several dozen items of jewellery, ranging from costume jewellery to expensive designer pieces. 'This is everything you've brought me. You would bring me something almost twice a month.'

Violaine fingered the jewellery and looked up at Pierre, shaking her head. 'I'm sorry, I don't remember. It's all gone.'

'That's what's so interesting!' he cried, taking back the drawer. 'You make the most fascinating study.'

'But I didn't steal all of these, did I?'

'Yes, you did,' he replied soberly. 'Sex?' he went on, abruptly changing the subject.

'What do you mean, sex?'

'Where are you sexually? Have you memories of that?'

'Why are you asking that? I'm not going to tell you about my life with Édouard. What's come over you? You think I'm in any state for sex at the moment? Look at me!'

'I'm not talking about that. Forget it. We can talk about it next time.' After another pause he said, 'Sins.'

'Sins? What do you mean?'

'Your brain, Violaine, has forgotten your vices and sins. The jewellery, the clothes, smoking …'

Violaine did not know how to reply, and instinctively put her hand in her pocket where she discovered a ring set with a round stone. Inspector Tanche's ring. She closed her eyes, taking deep breaths.

'Pierre, a police inspector came to the office. She showed me a photo of two men killed by a bullet to the head, like in *Sugar Flowers* ... Pierre, I know those two men.'

PART II

'I've heard good things about you.'

This was how Charles had greeted Violaine as he welcomed her into his office at the publishing house, more than twenty years ago now. With his habitual smile, he invited Violaine to sit on the sofa before taking his place beside her. He ran his hand through the silver-streaked blond hair that fell over his brow then briskly smoothed down the little moustache that made him look like a British colonel. At almost sixty years of age, Charles was the fourth generation to run the family publishing house. Charles held every key and pass, every code to every door, gate and turnstile of the publishing world into which he had been born. Violaine was barely twenty and wore her hair long and loose, but it was her delicate features and green eyes that would help her to make her mark.

'I take it Bernard brought you back from Normandy with him? How clever of him to agree to that signing in Rouen! I always encourage my authors to take up invitations from booksellers,' Charles said with a knowing smile.

At the time, Violaine was working weekends at a large bookshop in Rouen, fitting shifts around her literature degree. The disadvantage, or advantage, of universities is their lack of concern for their students: if those enrolled on the course don't show up to lectures there's no admonishment, no letter home to the parents, no search party sent out. It's only at the end of the year that the consequences are felt, if you don't pass your last modules or turn up to your few exams.

University is the perfect place to pass under the radar – to go incognito. To disappear.

Violaine had entered the bookshop after reading an advert taped to the glass door: 'Bookseller wanted, enquire within'. Following a brief interview, she was taken on that week. Her salary and university grant were just enough to rent a tiny attic room in an apartment block in the old part of Rouen. She was soon put in charge of bookshop events. Violaine was a quick reader and enjoyed talking to authors, most of whom were more than happy to have a smiling, pretty young woman escort them around the bookshop.

Bernard Ballier was a bestselling historical novelist. Readers devoured his stories set in Henri IV's Paris or Murat's Naples and felt better informed afterwards, since everything he wrote, whether depicting great historical events or scenes of daily life, was the fruit of the scrupulous research for which he was renowned. It was a reputation built on a lie, however, since he was actually assisted by an entire team of students – paid peanuts – and historical consultants handsomely rewarded for their discretion. Yet this trade secret was known only to his publishers; his readers would never be any the wiser. Affable, sure of himself, and a consummate ladies' man, Bernard Ballier had rounded off his signing session at the bookshop by asking Violaine, 'Fancy dinner?' She had accepted and after an evening at Restaurant La Couronne they had walked the streets of Rouen until, sure enough, their footsteps led them to the entrance of the hotel where the writer was staying.

Two hours later, Ballier was propped up on the pillows of the king-size bed, drawing on his cigarette.

'You're a remarkable girl. I'd go so far as to say quite exceptional in every way. What a shame you don't live in Paris, we could have had a proper affair.'

'Take me with you,' Violaine replied, heading into the bathroom.

'What about your studies? Your work?'

'A literature degree? That's not going to get me anywhere. I don't want to teach. And as for the bookshop, I don't want to stay there my whole life. Will you take me? I just need to have a shower and get dressed and I'll be ready. Let's go,' she declared as casually as possible, but with a distinctly daring look in her eyes.

'How much do you earn? Where do you live?' Ballier played along, giddy at the idea of packing up his latest conquest with his luggage the next morning.

Violaine revealed her modest salary and described her lodgings as 'mouse-sized'.

'I can find you another mousehole. As for money, I've an idea.' He paused to let a puff of tobacco smoke disperse before asking, 'Have you ever heard of a readers' room?'

Charles was smiling as he said, 'Bernard would like me to hire you as a reader in our manuscripts department. We have a vacancy. Do you have any experience of reading manuscripts?'

Violaine shook her head.

'The aim of the game is to find the best writing, but that's not all ...' he added, stroking his moustache again.

'By which you mean ...?' asked Violaine.

'By which I mean ...' Charles went on calmly, 'that it's very disagreeable to see a rival publisher topping the bestseller lists with a novel we too received in manuscript form ...'

'And you didn't sign the author up because you didn't rate their work highly enough.'

'Exactly – very good. And that has happened too often recently.'

He frowned. 'What you need is a kind of radar, one that swings between literary quality and commercial potential. It's not easy, I'll grant you. You've come from a bookshop, perhaps you have a clearer idea than most of what I'm trying to say.'

'Very clear, yes.'

'In that case,' he said warmly, 'Bernard was right to send you my way.' He looked Violaine in the eye. 'You have to go fishing if you want to find pearls.' He smiled. They both fell silent before Charles added, 'I'll be frank: what does a pretty girl like you see in Bernard Ballier?'

Violaine appeared to search for the answer on the ceiling before her gaze fell on Charles.

'He was able to bring me to Paris. And he's got money.'

'Now that's what I call honesty – I like it!' exclaimed Charles. 'And those are the only reasons you slept with him?'

'Yes,' Violaine replied matter-of-factly. 'If you like, I can sleep with you too.'

Charles sat wide-eyed before bursting out laughing.

'I can tell I'm going to like you, Mademoiselle Lepage. But not in that way,' he clarified. 'I'll let you into a secret, not that it is one.' He leant towards her and whispered in her ear, 'I like boys.'

'Shame – you're much better-looking than Bernard.'

'Thank you, my dear,' Charles replied, flattered, pushing his hair off his brow.

The rating system of the manuscript service soon became the language of Violaine's everyday life: numerous squares, a few moons and a sun that was to shine very brightly indeed upon its release, putting smiles on the faces of Charles and every member of the accounts department. Her arrival in the readers' room had not caused any ill feeling among her colleagues. Violaine was living in a studio flat belonging to Bernard Ballier which he went to occasionally to write, away from his wife and children. Since Violaine had come to Paris, he had felt the need to work in peace rather more often. After a year, Ballier and Violaine's relationship began to sour. He was annoyed at the way she relied on him to keep giving her handouts, while she resented him keeping her cloistered away at his pleasure. Eventually Ballier ended it and gave her two months to move out.

'I can't stay in the manuscript service or in Paris. I have to move back to Rouen,' she announced to Charles one morning.

'Out of the question,' was Charles's calm yet firm response. 'Have you lost your protector?' he added, smoothing his moustache.

'You could say that,' Violaine said vaguely. 'This city is too expensive, I can't afford to live here, Charles. I need to find a job ...'

'You've got a job here,' he cut in.

'You know very well I can't live off it, still less pay rent.'

'Come and live with me, then,' Charles said decisively. Then he returned to the letter he was writing.

'Sorry?'

'Two hundred and fifty square metres,' he reeled off without looking up. 'A duplex apartment with views of the Seine and the Institut de France. Will that do? I live on my own, it's too big. You can take a quarter for yourself. Take the afternoon off; we're going to the hairdresser's. I think a shoulder-length bob would suit you wonderfully.'

Violaine looked at him, unable to muster a response. More than the words, which brooked no argument, it was their calm delivery that stunned her. As if Charles had prepared for this conversation long ago, as if he had known all along what was going to happen. He had finished his letter with his swirly signature, his hand moving gracefully up and down on the page. Then he looked up at her.

'It's time we made something of you, Violaine.'

Charles had chosen himself a daughter in the same way he picked authors. Sometimes he poached them from rival publishers. Often it worked, but sometimes his efforts ended in failure: the authors simply didn't want to leave their publisher and trusted editor, and Charles's chequebook, promises of a prime place on the list and a full PR campaign were not enough to persuade them. At the end of the lunch, everyone shook hands, remained on good terms and promised to meet again sometime. Those who had refused his offer sometimes changed their minds a few years later. A schedule is not set in stone, anything might one day be possible. Charles excelled at the delicate art of leaving all doors open, to allow the winds of destiny to sweep in.

In a former life, Charles had been married and had a daughter, Charlotte. That life had long since come to an end. Upon the death of his father, Charles had taken advantage of his new-found status as sole heir to the publishing business to set his life in order, starting by admitting his preference for men. He and his wife divorced and, despite having been granted a generous settlement, she refused to see him again and did everything in her power to drive him and his daughter apart. She excelled herself, to the extent that Charlotte went on to put as much distance as possible between herself and her mother, taking off as a teenager to live far away from her parents and from France. She backpacked from Bali to Vietnam by way of Latin America, partying in open-air squats in far-off places, taking all manner of drugs and dancing to electro beats at late-night raves. She only returned to Paris once or twice a year to have lunch with her parents – separately – mainly to ask for money, for which they had both given up asking her to account. The years of hard living eventually took their toll on her body, which was found lifeless on a far-flung beach one morning, surrounded by beer cans and used syringes.

'A failure,' was Charles's matter-of-fact summary of his daughter's story. When she put her suitcase down in the hall of the apartment, Violaine had no idea she would be staying for ever.

She had swapped her part-time job in a bookshop in Rouen for a place at the heart of the Paris publishing scene. Living with Charles was like inhabiting the fountain from which the stream of literature flowed. With no prior discussion and with surprising ease, each carved out their own place in the apartment. Violaine occupied half of the first floor while Charles took the other, along with the upper level and terrace.

The pair would always retain an element of mystery for one another. Their willingness to respect one another's private worlds, to keep the ghosts of the past buried and to live only in the present sealed their unique bond. Violaine never mentioned or visited Normandy and Charles did not ask why. For his part, he never referred to his daughter or wife and had only rarely mentioned 'Hervé', whose Studio Harcourt portrait took pride of place on the mantelpiece, and who remained the love of Charles's life, having chosen to end his own ten years earlier. Since then, Charles had led a solitary existence, enlivened only by visits from rent boys five or six times a year.

Eight years passed in this way, between the quiet of the apartment and the buzz of literary events.

'Sleep with whomever you like, but don't bring any of our authors back here. This is our home,' Charles had warned.

If Violaine had lovers, some of whom remained on the scene longer than others, she always respected their pact. Though many of the publishing house's authors went to great pains to try to seduce her, none succeeded, during those years, in knowing Violaine intimately.

The book world looked upon this odd couple with a mixture of curiosity and puzzlement. The old hands laughed off Charles's conquest with veiled references to his preferences, while the less seasoned players were left perplexed, variously taking Violaine for Charles's daughter, wife, mistress, niece or intern.

During the fourth year, when Violaine found her fifth sun-worthy manuscript in the readers' room, Charles told her, 'And now you're going to publish it. You're ready to become an editor. Come on, let's go to La Coupole to celebrate.'

He liked to compare the literary world to a large fish tank, like the one in his office on the upper level of the apartment, three metres long and a metre and a half tall, in which at least sixty fish swam as if floating in zero gravity. Some nights after dinner, he and Violaine would sip green Chartreuse and watch the silent spectacle of the slow-moving creatures.

'Look closely. They're not all swimming at the same height. All in the same element, but not at the same level.'

Indeed, some followed a constant horizontal line, never encountering the fish swimming twenty centimetres above or below them.

'They're like our authors – each swimming at their own level according to sales figures and reputation.'

He even named some of the fish after writers he published. Smaller, almost neon species with flashes of blue, and red bellies, moved together in a shoal, whirling cloud-like from left to right, top to bottom, performing clever choreography they seemed to have perfected by telepathy.

'Those are the writers trying to get published,' Charles chuckled. 'They all appear alike, but one of them is head and shoulders above the rest. Which is it? The whole art of publishing lies in picking that fish out of the crowd. Isn't that so, Violaine?'

Violaine agreed. Some fish hid among the seaweed and aquatic plants for hours, even whole days. 'They're writing. They're cutting themselves off from the world to work, going incommunicado – like our authors,' she said, and Charles was delighted to welcome her into the game.

With all eyes on them, the wondrous fish lived quietly selfish lives. Keeping themselves to themselves, each playing their own role, they rarely communicated with their peers, just spending their days swimming endlessly back and forth behind the thick glass. They all seemed to have such busy schedules that the days were not long enough to fit everything in. Occasionally some would mysteriously disappear. Ill or imprudent, they had been eaten by others overnight. Two or three times a year, Charles would visit a specialist shop in order to buy a specimen of a species no longer represented in the tank – or even a new species he had heard about and had never owned before. He would come home carrying a plastic bag filled with air and water and proceed to release the new fish, fascinated by their first wriggling movements and even more so by their ability to adapt to their new home.

Now the fish tank was empty. Violaine had filled it with shells collected on holidays or bought at flea markets, their pearly sheen glimmering under the fluorescent lights. If she looked at it long enough, she sometimes imagined it filled with water again, teeming with fish swimming in every direction at different speeds. And she heard herself asking Charles, 'What about me? Which one am I?' He would always reply, 'You'll find out soon enough.'

*

Silent as Charles's fish but every bit as voracious, the other editors followed news of Violaine's promotion to their ranks with interest. The kindly ones saw it as a welcome injection of fresh blood, while others waited for her to trip up. She never did. Though she was pleased to have her own office – albeit a modest, windowless one – Violaine could not help missing the readers' room and the free-floating hours spent reading the first pages of a newly opened manuscript, seeking out the style, the talent and the magic of an author she was discovering for the first time. After publishing two acclaimed novels which bolstered her reputation as an editor, she began to receive manuscripts addressed to her personally. Most were sadly only worthy of a square, moons were rare occurrences and if the sun failed to shine on paper, it still hung high in the early summer sky.

On Thursdays, Violaine made a ritual of rounding off her lunch break with a walk around the Jardin du Luxembourg, finishing with a detour to the tennis courts where Charles played twice-weekly matches with his teacher or another player who could match his racket skills. She would give him a little wave through the railings and Charles would raise his eyebrows as if he was surprised to see her and swing his racket grandly as if ceremoniously inviting her to watch him play the next shots. He was always impeccably dressed in white and pale blue, with his floppy hair held back by a sweatband. That day, Violaine waved as usual through the bars. Charles feigned surprise for the hundredth time, swung his racket and returned to the back of the court. Service. Forehand drive, backhand, forehand. Point. 'Bravo!' shouted Violaine, clapping. Charles smiled and returned to the baseline. Service. Forehand, forehand, backhand, then, approaching the net, with one swift, precise movement he stopped his opponent's ball and volleyed it

94

across the court onto the white line. Point. Charles returned to the back of the court to play match point on his serve. He bounced the ball several times before throwing it up in the air, then he stretched backwards and smoothly swung his racket behind his back, preparing to strike the ball. He stopped mid movement, the yellow ball suspended in the blue sky like a second sun, and he fell to the ground.

The paramedics tried desperately to revive him. Kneeling beside him, the blood drained from her face, Violaine watched the defibrillator pads shock the unconscious publisher's chest. In vain.

'Damnit, we're losing him,' whispered the paramedic monitoring his pulse.

'Increase the voltage, Manu!' shouted another.

'For God's sake, J.P., what do you think I'm doing?'

Violaine had moved back and sat cross-legged on the tramlines. The same spot where Charles's last ball had landed, winning him the point. She ran her fingers along the white paint. Then she curled up, her head in her lap, and closed her eyes. The paramedics' words seemed far away, as if the summer wind had carried them to the other side of the park.

'Guys, who's going to talk to the daughter?'

'Karim?'

'It's always me …'

'Yeah, but you're good at talking.'

Panic had given way to silence, meaning it was over. Violaine sensed someone next to her, heavy shoes followed by a body kneeling beside her. She half opened her eyes to the sombre face of a gentle-looking boy with short brown hair, even younger than she was. He placed his hand on hers.

'You know why I'm here … I'm sorry, we couldn't resuscitate your father. We tried everything, but it wasn't enough. He's gone … but he didn't suffer. It was very sudden. I know this is really hard. This is a really shitty day.'

Violaine nodded. 'Yes, you're right, it's a really shitty day.'

The paramedic stayed with her for a few minutes without saying anything, before clearing his throat.

'Is there someone you can call? We can't stay here …'

Violaine took out her Nokia and dialled the number for Thérèse, Charles's secretary.

'Violaine!' she exclaimed cheerfully. 'We've been looking everywhere for Charles. Are you with him?'

'Thérèse …' Violaine began tonelessly, before bursting into tears.

'Oh my God,' murmured Thérèse. 'Where are you?'

Liblivre, Charles's partner, called a special board meeting to decide the company's short-term strategy following the sudden death of the publishing icon. An interim chief executive was appointed and the will was formally opened. Charles had left instructions for the head of Liblivre to take over his publishing house, as well as stipulating that the two editorial directors should remain in charge. A new clause, added a year earlier, was discovered: upon Charles's death, Violaine Lepage was to become third in command of the editorial department, and would be put in charge of the readers' room under the title 'Head of Manuscript Services', a new position created especially for her.

The announcement in front of the entire staff caused something of a stir. Some were reassured to see a little bit of Charles living on through Violaine, while others were not best pleased at the 'Dauphine', as she was called, cementing her power by controlling one of the most important areas of the publishing house: the readers' room. When the board approved her appointment by a majority vote Violaine shut herself in a room and took Charles's phone out of her pocket, scrolling through the contacts until she got to 'M'. She had taken it when Charles's body was transferred to the morgue, handing all his personal effects over to his family, with the exception of the phone.

One of Charles's eccentricities consisted in adding the full names of dead authors to his contacts list, complete with made-up phone numbers. Thus, among his impressive list of contacts, which contained every name in French publishing and a quarter of those in the business worldwide, were such names as Guy de Maupassant: 06 78 65 45, Gustave Flaubert: 06 56 33, Charles Baudelaire, André Breton, Emily Brontë, Louis-Ferdinand Céline, F. Scott Fitzgerald, Victor Hugo, Joris-Karl Huysmans, Lautréamont, Pierre Loti, Anaïs Nin, Georges Perec, Marcel Proust, George Sand, Georges Simenon, Stendhal, Virginia Woolf ...

At times of intense boredom or melancholy, he would select a name and a message would appear on-screen saying, 'Calling: Guy de Maupassant'. After a few rings a voice would answer.

'Hello?'

'Guy, is that you?' asked Charles.

'Sorry, you've got the wrong number,' the voice would reply.

'My apologies.'

Charles would hang up, but not without those few seconds with the writer's name on his screen having filled him with almost hysterical joy. No sooner had he put the phone down than he would save another random number in the phone book, ready to call another Maupassant. After several years living together, Charles had shared his quirk with Violaine, who seized upon the idea with gusto. Several times a year, the two of them would play what they called 'Dial a friend'. While dining together, or finding themselves alone in a taxi, Charles would suddenly turn towards her.

'How about calling a friend?' he would say.

'OK,' Violaine replied.

'You choose.'

'Let's give Rimbaud a ring,' she would suggest.

Charles scrolled through the names to find the poet's mobile number. During these moments, he had a twinkle in his eye, like a little boy relishing doing something of which he knows his parents will disapprove. Violaine would sit close to him to listen in to whichever poor soul was being bothered by the call. The conversation always ended quickly, or else he left a long message, but of course no one ever called him back.

On the sombre day which marked the beginning of her ascendancy at the publishing house, but also the end of Charles's era, Violaine felt the urge to call a 'friend'. She clicked on the name of the author of *In Search of Lost Time* and 'Calling: Marcel Proust' came up on-screen.

After a few rings came 'Hello?'

'Marcel?' asked Violaine.

'Speaking,' a voice replied softly.

Violaine abruptly hung up. A few days later, she received a call from Charles's lawyer. Summoned to an office in the sixth arrondissement, whose windows looked out – ironically enough – on the Luxembourg tennis courts, she learned that she was the sole beneficiary of Charles's will. According to Charles's last handwritten amendments, added two years earlier, he was leaving his apartment and fortune to her. His ex-wife launched an unsuccessful appeal and an agreement was reached with one of Charles's brothers. Being unrelated to Charles, there was a hefty inheritance tax bill to pay, yet Violaine found herself nonetheless, at barely thirty, never having to worry about money again, and the apartment in which she had set down her suitcase eight years previously now belonged to her.

A few months later, she decided to change the shelves in the readers' room and Édouard was shaking her hand and saying tonelessly, 'You're not at all as I imagined.'

Sophie Tanche took a deep breath. At the same time, one of the forensics officers finally turned the key in the ignition. The engine went quiet and the headlights went out. Since arriving on the scene at 5 a.m., the engine had been humming constantly and exhaust fumes had filled the air. How many litres of petrol had the Renault got through while the engine had been on? Perhaps an entire tankful, Sophie guessed, which led her to thinking it was about time she filled up her own car, and got the horribly squeaky right windscreen wiper fixed. She drove these thoughts from her mind and forced herself to focus on the scene in front of her: the dirt road, the entrance to the forest, the car, the body.

The forensics officers were moving about in hooded white overalls and masks like the ones surgeons wear, as if protecting themselves from radiation. Inspector Tanche had made this observation numerous times at crime scenes. The brain is on maximum alert but briefly focuses on insignificant details to transport you far away from the here and now, filling your mind with the most mundane thoughts – this time petrol and a windscreen wiper.

'Thanks!' shouted Sophie, and the technician in white, of whom she could see only his eyes above the mask, gave her a thumbs up to show that he too was happier now that damned engine had been switched off. A young woman, also dressed in white, was moving slowly around them, filming the scene on a digital camera. Carefully placing one foot in front of the other, she circled the body, taking great care not to shake the lens. Sophie couldn't remember the girl's name – Valérie or Virginie or Nathalie was in charge of taking pictures of crime scenes while her colleagues went round taking swabs. She always took very good images – slow, precise: horrifying. She was said to keep copies of the pictures and put them to hypnotic music like Barber's Adagio for Strings or Angelo Badalamenti's theme for *Mulholland Drive*.

Sophie's phone had rung at 4.40 a.m. that morning, rousing her from a bad dream which she promptly forgot.

'It's starting again,' Chief Superintendent Malier had stated plainly.

'Is it the taxi driver?' Sophie asked, sitting up in bed.

'Got it in one. So, this theory of yours about the book that's up for some prize – I'm going to need you to get hold of that author, because this has gone beyond a joke, and I'm going to have to put in a report about this, Sophie. I'm two months off retirement, I've been on the squad thirty-eight years and I'm not about to get myself chucked out in my last sixty days. Got it?'

'Got it, sir.'

'Alain's on his way. He'll pick you up.'

Eight days had passed since she had asked Violaine for Camille Désencres's details. After lengthy contemplation of the waxed parquet floor of her office, Violaine had looked up at her.

'I don't have them. I don't know who Camille is,' she admitted.

'Are you having me on?'

'No. All I've got is an email address. And Camille Désencres has stopped replying.'

'You have no idea who wrote *Sugar Flowers*?'

'No. The contract was returned by post. I've never met the author. If this book wins the Goncourt, I can't go and accept the prize without an author. It'll be the end of my career, Inspector.'

'Madame Lepage, I'm not here to talk about a literary prize. This is a criminal investigation.'

'I can't help you. I can't even help myself ...' was the only answer Violaine could give.

Sophie had quickly brushed her short hair and pulled on her clothes without even visiting the bathroom. In the kitchen, she put coffee on. Everything about this house was too big: the kitchen, the living room, the bedroom, the bed. It was a home made for two, if not more. It no longer made sense to be living in a large detached house, yet Sophie couldn't quite bring herself to sell it.

During the drive, her partner, Alain Massard, briefly described how the body had been discovered. An eighteen-year-old boy driving his father's car had brought a girl he'd met at a party to the scene at around four in the morning.

'I guess he was hoping to give her one in the car.'

'Yes, I gathered that, thank you,' Sophie shot back.

'So anyway,' Alain replied, 'they get to the forest and find this car with its lights on and a figure kneeling in front of it. They could have turned round there and then, but the kid got out to take a closer look before calling the police.'

'As calmly as that?'

'Yep. You know, kids these days grow up binge-watching crime series on Netflix. The night couldn't have worked out better for him – OK, he didn't get laid, but now he's got her thinking he's a total hero.'

Sophie raised her eyebrows and pouted disapprovingly.

'I'm serious, Sophie. They probably wish they'd taken a selfie with the body and posted it on Instagram.'

'Please, Alain, stop!' Sophie cut him off. 'I don't want to hear it.'

'All right … Inspector Maigret. Speaking of which,' he went on, 'I reread Simenon this weekend. Wow, have those stories dated. They don't hold up at all any more. With DNA and mobile phones, all the mysteries would have been solved by page 40.' Sophie made no reply. 'So what about your *Sugar Flowers* and the book's editor – still think they're in the picture?'

'Yes,' was the extent of her reply.

Sophie took a packet of Marlboro Reds from the pocket of her leather biker jacket and flicked the lighter. The first puff travelled through her lungs and she felt the blood pumping faster through her veins. Tobacco was truly one of the filthiest inventions on earth, yet she told herself despondently she would never be able to give up cigarettes.

'Inspector!' one of the white-coated men shouted at her.

Sophie raised her hand apologetically and stepped back; Forensics couldn't stand police officers lighting cigarettes close to crime scenes, spreading microparticles and potentially leaving fag ends on the ground. Sophie moved still further away, sat on a tree trunk and took her copy of *Sugar Flowers* from her bag. She opened it on a page marked with a pink Post-it on which she had written the number 3, and took a drag on her cigarette.

> At night, when forest life continues without men, when animals domestic and wild reign over the land, prey and predators play their death matches. The losers are counted in the morning's dried blood. There will be a loser in the forest tonight. In the car's headlights there will be a man on his knees with a hole in his head. The souls of the hedgehogs, grass snakes and cats squashed under

the wheels of his car will float around him. He will
be the hedgehog, the grass snake and the cat. He
will know perfectly well why he is there.

Sophie closed her eyes and opened them again on the scene of
the crime. The taxi had stopped at the edge of the forest. Four
metres from the headlights, a bald man in his fifties wearing black
jeans and a khaki shirt was on his knees, frozen stiff in death, his
head tipping forward, a dark hole between his eyes. The bullet
must have ripped through his pharynx and glottis, as two trails of
dry blood ran down from the corners of his mouth. Marc Fournier,
the taxi driver, son of the former mayor of Bourqueville, had taken
his last fare the previous night. Sophie stubbed out her cigarette
in the little jam pot she used as a pocket ashtray. She stood up and
took a few steps towards the body. There was an expression of
something like resignation on his face, a million miles away from
the horrified looks on the faces of his two friends, Sébastien Balard
and Damien Perchaude, a year earlier. Marc Fournier worked for
himself. An ordinary, divorced, childless bloke who was, in his
own words, only interested in hunting and cars. He belonged to
a small tuning club, along with a dozen or so other chrome and
valve fanatics. She had been to see him a year ago, after the double
murder. He had been stunned, shaking his head from side to side
and murmuring, 'It can't be true' – it ended up getting on her
nerves. Marc Fournier was no great mind, but he had retreated
into a state of stupefied denial, and the inspector had failed to glean
anything from the interview. No, he had no idea what motive there
could have been for his friends' killing. She remembered when
she asked her last question – 'Do you feel threatened, Monsieur
Fournier?' – he had looked up blankly and replied, 'Me? Who by?'

Sophie took in the man's fixed, glassy gaze. He seemed to be
watching a blade of grass bending under the weight of a ladybird.

She brought her finger to it and the dome-shaped insect carefully climbed on. Sophie counted three black dots on its orange wings and off it flew.

Alain knelt beside her and, with a sigh, pointed to Fournier's head.

'To think that everything's in there: the film of the murder, the soundtrack, the motive, the murderer, everything. And we can't get to it.'

'Yes,' murmured Sophie. 'That's why cops were invented. So, same weapon, I imagine?'

'Yes. The bullet came out through the back of the neck, just above his collar. Luger P08, still just as untraceable. Same goes for the phone.'

'Tell me,' sighed Sophie.

'The call for the ride came from a burner phone.'

Sophie shook her head. A burner phone was a cheap disposable mobile that could be topped up with pre-pay cards from newsagents or online. Drug dealers used them and then got rid of them in public bins. Weeks of investigation would lead at best to a second-hand phone salesman with no memory of a transaction that may have dated back several months, and which would doubtless have been paid in cash.

'DNA?' asked Sophie.

'Forensics are on it. You can imagine how much DNA gets left in a taxi. Dozens of traces, at least. Bits of hair and nail – it'll be a zoo in there.'

'There won't be any DNA,' Sophie declared, 'or at least none that's any use to us, and no mobile phone either. There'll be nothing,' she concluded, standing up. 'You see, Alain, Simenon does still hold water and the book doesn't stop at page 40.'

'Touché,' Alain conceded, smiling. 'So what exactly are we looking for?'

'We're looking for … Camille Désencres.' Sophie took a fresh cigarette out of the packet and flicked her lighter. 'A man, a woman, a writer, a killer, a murderess. I don't know how, but everything stems from one bizarre place: a thirty-square-metre room in which people are paid to read books that don't yet exist.'

'What is this place?'

Sophie blew out a puff of blue smoke.

'The readers' room.'

Sunlight was filtering through the branches onto the dry ground of the Jardin du Luxembourg, leaving scattered patches of brightness which moved with the wind. Violaine liked these early November days, when the cold of the coming winter begins to descend on Paris. The city sky may still be perfectly blue at this time of year – not so the sky above publishers, which is filled with clouds, gusty winds and even the odd lightning strike. The literary prize season lasts barely three months, its weather systems are more unpredictable than a long-range forecast and each editor lives in his or her own microclimate: radiant sunshine and unexpected boom times for some, icy showers and disastrous sales figures for others.

For Violaine's publishing house, *Winter of Lakes* had made only a fleeting appearance on the longlist of the Prix Renaudot; *Self-portrait of Misfortune* had missed out on the Académie Française award by a whisker; *A Meeting* was no longer in the running for the Femina. *Sugar Flowers*, still up for the Goncourt, was the last one standing. Around lunchtime, Violaine would receive a call or text from one of the judges to let her know whether the novel was to figure among the four finalists. The judges, led by the president of the Académie Goncourt, Bernard Pivot, would give the titles of the shortlisted books to the press that day, and the eventual winner would be announced exactly seven days later, when the final round of voting would be held upstairs at Restaurant Drouant, following a tradition that dated back over a century. For a publishing house, an author and their editor, winning the Goncourt is on a par with reaching the World Cup final for a football team's manager, coach and country. Without the global TV audience figures, of course – though the Goncourt is also screened live around the world. You need only observe the buzz of journalists and the sea of satellite dishes set up outside the famous restaurant on Place Gaillon an hour before the results to have some idea of what's to come inside those walls sixty minutes later. Before the results, the journalists, literary critics and guests assembled downstairs in the restaurant can only wait and make predictions, like a party HQ waiting for the results on election night. Then the secretary-general comes downstairs, declares the votes cast and reveals the victor. And then it's time to wait again, for the winner's arrival. In order to save them from the crush of photographers and hordes of radio and TV reporters holding out their microphones, as soon as the winning author emerges from the car booked by their publisher, they are escorted by police officers on the forty-metre walk to the entrance of the restaurant. It's a scrum of passes, press accreditations, interview requests, champagne and euphoria. The winner appears at the first-floor window of the restaurant and the photographers who've stayed out on the pavement snap away. The battle is over.

Violaine had witnessed this fanfare only three times in her twenty-year career at the publishing house, and never for a book she had edited. Far from the buzz of the restaurant, back at the office, time stands still: the MD, the editor and the writer sit in stony silence, waiting for the phone to ring – or not. Not only is the Goncourt the most prestigious of all the prizes, it also guarantees an incredible print run and sales to match – at least four hundred thousand copies, sometimes far more. From the moment the award is announced, the winner can clear their diary for the coming year, or take a sabbatical if they're working: a huge tour of French bookshops and libraries will be organised, later spilling out into Europe and the wider world once the translations are published.

The Goncourt-winning title is bought, read and given as a present at dinners in town and family gatherings until Christmas. Put simply, it's a goldmine – the perfect combination of literary recognition and commercial success.

'Can't you sleep?' Édouard mumbled that morning, turning to face his wife in bed.

Violaine had her eyes wide open and the morning light was seeping in through the gap in the heavy red-and-blue paisley curtains which dated from Charles's era and which she refused to change. A bright ray of light fell on the bridge of her nose, highlighting her perfect profile.

'No,' Violaine replied.

Édouard adjusted the sheets, propping himself up on one elbow against the pillow.

'Thinking about the Goncourt? The shortlist comes out today, doesn't it?' he said, reaching towards her lit-up face. He placed his index finger just above her forehead, a centimetre above her skin, and began tracing the line which ran down to her eyebrows and rose at the tip of her nose before falling to her lips and onwards to the curve of her chin.

'Imagine if it's shortlisted,' Violaine said, without taking her eyes off the ceiling.

'Imagine if it wins,' Édouard replied. 'Then what will you do? Without an author …'

Édouard's hand now floated above Violaine's breasts, which he could make out through the sheets.

'I don't know …' she murmured. 'I'd rather not think about it,' she sighed.

Violaine had pulled the sheets down to reveal her breasts, and Édouard's hand had gently settled there like a dog waiting to be petted.

'Touch me,' Violaine whispered.

Édouard slowly opened his hand to place his thumb on her right nipple and his little finger on her left. The slight movement of his wrist brought a sigh to Violaine's lips.

'And the cop looking into those crimes …?' Édouard went on.

'I don't know,' Violaine said after a few seconds of silence.

'She's crazy, isn't she? I mean, I think she's crazy,' he added, stroking her breasts and then running his hand down her belly. He brought his face close to Violaine's and whispered in her ear, 'She's crazy about you. She just wants to meet you, or to get herself published, that's it, she's trying to get published …'

'Stop it, Édouard,' Violaine said sharply, before pressing her husband's hand between her thighs. Her green eyes opened beneath him. 'Take me,' she ordered with a gasp.

Making love with her leg in plaster wasn't exactly easy, but in fact it was less acrobatic than she might have imagined. What exactly happens during the act of love? Which part of yourself lets go, as if drugged into abandonment, and which other part remains hyper alert, paying close attention to every breath, every touch and movement, and watches in fascination as pleasure washes over the other's body? The two parts come together at the moment of climax, which rises up like the sudden, shining solution to an equation you have been feeling for through touch, kisses, bites, positions and words uttered breathlessly. It seems the hormone associated with the state of love is called luliberin. The brain releases it without warning when we fall in love, and it's thanks to luliberin that the beloved is suddenly endowed with every possible attribute, becoming the source of all pleasure and all possibilities. The biologist Jean-Didier Vincent explored love in an essay over four hundred pages long entitled *The Biology of Passions*. Several years later, his wife published a more accessible version for a general readership, *How Do We Fall in Love?* The loving state brought on by luliberin lasted ninety days, according to scientists. The previous year, Violaine had shared this radical finding with Édouard when she came across it in an article on love in literature in *Le Figaro Littéraire* which quoted Lucy Vincent's essay. Immersed in a feature in *Architectural Digest* about a rich Scotsman's castle renovations, he had looked up from his reading and said distractedly, 'Oh, really? Then I must be an interesting case – the doctors ought to study me. Because for me it's lasted since I came to fit the shelves in the readers' room.'

Violaine chose to sit on one of the famous metal seats in the park. She leant on the cane she had bought that morning as she passed the row of antiques shops on the way to her office. The antiques dealer had been in the window, laying out various objects: a snuffbox made of horn or ivory, a corozo darning egg, small cases made of mother-of-pearl, a cast-iron key and a clay pipe. He moved them fractionally forwards or backwards, or rapidly removed them from the window. Then he set down a very lovely cane made from burnished boxwood with an ivory and silver handle and a cartouche bearing the initials 'M.P.'

Violaine studied the stick carefully, assessing its size, before pushing open the door to the shop. Ten minutes later, she walked out of the shop and headed up the road leaning firmly on the beautiful age-polished cane, and threw the hospital-issue aluminium and grey plastic one into a bin. Tourists passed, silhouetted by the sun, occasionally stopping to take photos with their smartphones. Some holding ridiculous extending sticks grouped together and took selfies. Other figures crossed the park more quickly – regular visitors or residents of the neighbourhood. These people called the park by its nickname: le Luco. The sunlight warmed her face and a sweet sense of calm washed over her, a little like the minutes following the morning's lovemaking with Édouard. If she listened hard, she could hear tennis balls being struck on the courts, like the muffled ticking of a clock. When a man sat in the metal seat beside her, Violaine turned to him and smiled.

His gaze was as tender and kindly as ever. Those dark circles under his eyes, that impeccably combed moustache ... He took off a grey felt hat to reveal jet-black hair. He was wearing his sealskin coat. His hands were gloved, the right hand resting on the metal armrest while the left gently stroked the gleaming pelt of the coat.

'This is your cane,' Violaine declared softly.

'It is indeed.' Marcel Proust nodded.

'I knew it.' Violaine smiled. 'It's one of the mysteries of literature,' she went on.

'I beg your pardon?'

'Your voice. What it sounded like. There are no recordings, nothing ...'

'It seems the mystery is solved, is it not?'

'Yes ...'

Violaine held out her hand. Proust nimbly took off his pale leather gloves and took Violaine's hand in his. How warm and soft they were, these hands which spent every day writing, with nib and Indian ink, that cathedral of literature with its cast of more than two thousand characters: *In Search of Lost Time*. He had carried on writing until it cost him his already fragile health – until it cost him his life. Though his body may have given up and his biological life come to an end, Proust had been reincarnated in his book the moment it was printed. Through the mystery of the Eucharist, the body of Christ is present in the bread and wine during Communion with the faithful; Marcel Proust, like all writers of genius, had succeeded – and he more than any other – in this transmutation which is the very essence of literature: a spirit and soul embodied in a rectangle of bound paper, living on after them. For ever. Violaine closed her eyes and brushed Marcel's moustache and lips with her fingertips.

'France Info, it's midday and this is the news with Nathalie Andrieu.' Violaine jumped. Her phone, which she had programmed to alert her to news flashes, had just automatically tuned in to the radio. She turned to the seat next to her and the bright sunlight made her screw up her eyes. The seat was empty.

'We start with some news just in – the shortlist for the Prix Goncourt has been revealed,' the voice of the journalist continued. 'The four finalists announced by the Académie Goncourt are: Pierre Demerrieux for *The Fickle*, Bruno Tardier for *Our Empty Childhoods*, Agnès Maryan for *The Unfinished Castle* and Camille Désencres for *Sugar Flowers*.'

'Of course you know who it is …' Pascal gave a cool business-like smile. Violaine had been called into his office shortly after the shortlist announcement. During the walk back through the Jardin du Luxembourg to the publishing house, she had received no fewer than three phone calls from the police inspector, none of which she had answered.

Violaine stared back at Pascal.

'Of course I know who it is,' she whispered.

Pascal let out a sigh of relief.

'Thank goodness. For a while there, you had me believing your tale of the phantom author. Imagine if we win – would we have gone to pick up the prize at Drouant without an author?!'

Without taking his eyes off her, Pascal chewed the end of his Montblanc ballpoint.

'Well then, who is it?'

'Not yet, it's too soon,' replied Violaine.

'Give me a clue, at least: is it a man or a woman?'

Violaine appeared to look for the answer in the bookshelves lining the wall.

'A woman,' she said at last.

You have three new messages.

Message received at 10.45 a.m.:

'Madame Lepage, it's Inspector Tanche, Sophie Tanche. I have a problem … Two crimes were committed a year ago – I showed you the photos when we met in Paris. Madame Lepage, another crime took place last night and it matches page 147 of the book you published. Madame, I don't think you quite understand that you're involved in a criminal investigation – you, your publishing house and your manuscript service.

'You told me you didn't know who your author was and just gave me an email address. I'm afraid that won't do. I think you're hiding something from me. I think you know who wrote the book. I'm coming to Paris, I'm on my way. I'm going to ask to see your diary, along with those of everyone else connected with your readers' room.'

Message received at 11.37 a.m.:

'I left you a message an hour ago. Madame Lepage, when the police leave you a message, most people call back within ten minutes.'

'I'm just coming into Paris, I'm heading for your publishing house. I haven't heard anything from you. I'm going to ask to be taken to your office and I'll wait for you there for as long as it takes. I heard on the way that your book has made the shortlist of the Goncourt. Congratulations. Now don't you dare tell me you don't know who wrote it.'

Inviting an author to lunch is one of the publishing world's great rituals. Authors receive an invitation four or five times a year. Since there are many authors in one publishing house, that means a lot of lunches. Editors feed their authors like fat misanthropic cats they're hoping to butter up and make purr. The goal of a literary lunch is to maintain friendly relations with the author. But also – and above all – to find out if he or she is working and has made progress with the manuscript for which an advance has been paid by bank transfer. Between those who write too much and those who write too little, between the 'ink cows' who'd like nothing better than to be published twice a year and those who might write one line on a good weekend, the contracts and advances are carefully distributed – along with the lunches. Some authors send pages to their editors regularly and want feedback before they continue, others disappear for months on end without a word, leaving their editors worried. Pascal paid close attention to this and had created a special Excel spreadsheet to keep tabs on authors: every three months, he wanted an update on where they were and what they were doing. The budget of the fiction department, which had a turnover of several million euros and employed a substantial number of staff, relied entirely on the inspiration and imagination of its authors – that is to say, on totally unpredictable elements.

Pascal had once summed it up with a simple question: 'What if those fools run out of ideas – then what?' No one had dared respond.

Several years earlier, one of the house's big authors had gone quiet. He had gone to India with the first half of a considerable advance. A private detective agency had had to be called in to track him down and discover that he had written not a single page of the book, which, by the way, was not supposed to have anything to do with India. The author's bad patch had provided the inspiration for a short novel, *Rubbed Out* – the story of a private detective looking for a writer who had run off with his advance. Written in three months on his return to France and boosted by glowing reviews, the novel shot to the top of the bestseller lists. The film adaptation starring Vincent Lindon had even earned the actor a César. If you looked at things clinically, the author had therefore been justified in duping his publisher and going to the other side of the world with his advance – if he hadn't done so, he would never have written the book which remained his biggest success to date. From initial idea to finished book, novels have lives of their own which elude even their authors.

Casually asking the author between starter and main how they're getting on with the next book is par for the course. Using crafty tactics to try to ascertain over dessert whether they really know how the story ends is another variation on the theme. It's not uncommon for an author to be asked to pull their socks up – a technique at which Violaine excelled and which she fully intended to deploy on François Mailfer, one of her authors who had had several bestsellers but had produced too little for her liking in recent years. The dining room of Rostand, looking out onto the Jardin du Luxembourg, was buzzing with the usual brasserie hubbub: a mixture of clinking cutlery, conversation and tinkling glasses.

'You've written nothing for three years,' Violaine began brusquely. 'You've been resting on your laurels, a TV series and ten translations in the offing. Is it too much to ask for you to write another novel, François?'

'I'm busy with my writing workshops.'

'You spend all your time in workshops. You're always talking about your students. Stop helping other people, François. If that's really what you want to do, go and work for an NGO.'

François Mailfer put down his kir and looked Violaine straight in the eye.

'I'm serious,' she went on. 'Stop worrying about everyone else. Writers are selfish people who only think about themselves, their books, their work. That's why they're impossible megalomaniacs who are a nightmare to work with, but at least they move forward – that's their strength, they make their own way in the world. Are you starved of affection? Start seeing a new woman, get a cat or a dog. Or a bird.'

'Did you really just say that?' the author replied coldly.

'Yes, I really did.'

'Steak with morels and crosnes in basil butter,' the waiter announced.

'Is it wrong to help people who want to write?' asked François as he poured wine into Violaine's glass.

'Yes, it is.'

'Violaine …' he sighed, rolling his eyes.

'It is wrong,' Violaine repeated as she attacked her beef. 'You're making them think they can become writers. You're allowing them to delude themselves. If they have talent, they don't need you to tell them what to do. There's no such thing as an undiscovered genius. All you're creating is unhappy people who will never get over not making it, because you led them to believe they could do it. You're creating bitterness, François. You're causing harm. Leave them all alone and write your books. Let them keep working their guts out and send their masterpieces to me in the readers' room. I'm the gatekeeper, François, not you.'

'That's crap!' he exclaimed, slamming his cutlery down on his plate so loudly that the two women at the next table jumped and turned towards him. 'Authors have come out of creative writing classes.'

'Very few ...' Violaine shot back, biting into a morel. 'And not from yours, in any case.'

'You're a very hard woman, Violaine. You always have been.'

'Yes, but deep down, because you're an intelligent man, you know I'm right.'

François Mailfer made no reply and concentrated on the beef.

'Good, isn't it?' Violaine asked lightly.

'I'm going to change editors.'

'You're abandoning me? You'd do that to a disabled woman? Shame on you, François, what a monster you are ...'

'You're the monster. How can you speak to me like that after everything we've been through?'

'Precisely. We've had success together. Which is precisely why we need to keep going.'

'That's not what I'm talking about,' the author replied curtly.

'What, then?'

'Us. Our history,' he went on, without taking his eyes off her.

'What history?' Violaine asked tonelessly.

'What history?!' he repeated ironically, shaking his head. 'A history of secret rendezvous, hotel rooms at provincial book fairs, even planes to foreign tours. Look,' he ordered, rolling up his sleeve to reveal a scar. 'I'll have the mark of your fingernails on my arm for life. I'd been warned: Violaine's like that, she'll seduce you, sleep with you and then one day she'll forget you. You've done the same to so many others, why would it be any different with me? Why do I run so many writing workshops? Maybe it's to forget you. To try ... Why are you looking at me like that, Violaine?'

Sophie's partner, Alain Massard, had been landed with the difficult task of informing Marc Fournier's relatives of his death. He usually managed to avoid being the one to give bad news, but this time Sophie was not going to let him get out of it: she was going straight back to Paris to see Violaine Lepage, the editor of *Sugar Flowers*, and ask every member of her team to account for their movements.

'Anyway, Fournier didn't have a wife or kids,' Sophie said shortly. 'That'll make things easier for you, won't it?'

Alain did not reply.

Worse even than finding a body was having to contact the victim's loved ones. First came the phone call. Alain drew from a series of stock phrases and took on an appropriately detached, almost military air: 'Hello, this is Inspector Massard from Rouen police. I need to see you as soon as possible. It's about ...' – here he would insert one of several variations: your wife, your daughter, your father, your son, your husband ...

At the other end of the line, there was always incomprehension followed by a pause. Whatever the circumstances, that moment always came, a second during which Alain could sense the rising panic and anxiety in a person who was still, for now, only a voice at the other end of a telephone. The question that followed also came in various guises, and was delivered with varying degrees of distress, but generally boiled down to: 'What happened?' Alain had his answer ready: 'Something very serious, but I'd like to tell you about it face to face. I'm on my way.'

In his view, you couldn't just blithely announce a death on the phone, catching someone off guard during lunch or even in the middle of the night. You had to give them a chance to prepare themselves for the worst, and the expression 'something very serious' allowed them to consider every eventuality, including death – and thus to contemplate the prospect of it. He had explained his method to a police psychologist during an assessment interview. 'You're right, Inspector. You clearly handle such situations with a great deal of care, which can't be said of all your colleagues,' the psychologist had said.

The next hurdle to get over was the intercom for a block of flats or the doorbell of an individual house. This was where things got complicated for Alain, because it was at this point that everything was about to change. Here he was, the bearer of terrible news, news which would devastate a family for ever. After he had spoken, nothing would ever be the same again. Behind the door he found the worried faces of women, men, sometimes children, watching him closely. He silently entered homes he should never have set foot in: plush drawing rooms filled with fine furnishings and family mementos, middle-class lounges with designer leather sofas and flat-screen TVs, or very meagre lodgings in which any attempt at decoration proved futile. Sometimes the smell of a scented candle hung in the air, or wafts of soup cooking in the kitchen. Each time, Alain felt he was intruding into happy, private spaces, gently placing a stick of dynamite on the family coffee table and, as everyone looked on, pressing the red button which would blow everything to pieces. When, at two in the morning, he had had to tell the parents of little Louise Fermaux, aged twelve, that the lifeless body of their daughter had been found in the boot of a car pulled over for a simple speeding offence, the mother had screamed so loudly that Alain had been unable to speak. No further words had passed his lips; he was paralysed at the sight of this woman on her knees in her dressing gown, her face twisted in pain, while her husband tried vainly to calm her down and the little dog yapped frantically around her. Alain had begun to shake and had placed his hands over his ears before curling up on their sofa, unable to move a muscle. He was signed off work for three days and prescribed powerful sedatives. The police doctor had diagnosed a panic attack and had given instructions that Alain should not be sent to inform next of kin of a death for the next several months.

Marc Fournier's case was a bit different. There was no point in going to his home, since he was the only one who lived there. No wife or child, as Sophie had pointed out. No known partner. An elder sister living in Italy, whom they were trying to reach. Marc Fournier was, however, the son of a former mayor of Bourqueville, who had served three terms during the nineties. Widowed, he had retired to his estate, the exact name of which no one seemed able to provide. The simplest solution was to ask the current mayor – in any case he would have to be informed of the discovery of a body in his district. The mayor's secretary asked Alain to wait.

'Monsieur le Maire will see you as soon as possible,' she added, before quickly exiting through a large doorway. Hearing her heels tapping on the parquet floor, Alain thought of his ex, Inès, whose buckled high-heeled sandals made the same sound. Since their break-up, he had sometimes heard the sound of them in his dreams and woken with a start. For the past three months he had been seeing Virginie, the forensics officer responsible for photographing crime scenes. Virginie was pretty and sweet-natured, said little and often responded to questions with nothing but a shy smile. You wouldn't imagine that Virginie, such a good girl, who kept herself to herself with her photos and videos, would be quite so enthusiastic in the bedroom. During these last three months, Alain had been going to her place every evening for a dinner that invariably ended in wild sessions on the living-room carpet. Little used to this daily pattern with previous partners, Alain realised he had lost no less than five kilos. For the moment, they had managed to keep their relationship quiet at work, and again this morning, at the taxi crime scene, they had pretended not to know one another. When Sophie asked him to remind her of 'the video girl's' name, Alain replied, 'Virginie, isn't it?'

The heels could be heard again returning.

'Monsieur le Maire will see you now, Inspector.'

Jean-François Combes was a very large man in his forties, with a double chin which he tried to hide under a greying beard. His ill-fitting navy suit made his shoulders look over-large, and his arms, emerging from the too-short sleeves, like flippers grafted onto his body. The combination of his excess weight, facial hair and flippers made him look much older than he really was. He stood up, hand outstretched.

'Good morning, Inspector. I heard the news,' he said sombrely. 'How dreadful,' he added, furrowing his brow. 'Fournier was the nicest man.'

Once again, Alain noted how the average person with even a passing acquaintance with those involved in a criminal investigation tends to heap praise upon them: the murderer is always described as a straightforward, ordinary neighbour, who kept themselves to themselves, yes, but helped people out in the neighbourhood, while the victim is invariably the finest of men, the pride and joy of his family and a most valued employee. He had never heard anyone say of a killer, 'I'm not surprised the bastard pulled a knife, he always was a piece of work,' or of a victim, 'He was just a complete idiot who never said hello, parked his car wherever he liked and was always yelling at his wife and kids.'

After a pause – intended to be solemn and profound – the mayor went on.

'That makes three in the area in less than a year.'

He raised his fist very deliberately, straightening three podgy fingers in turn:

'Perchaude, the notary' (thumb), 'Balard, who owned Thor' (index finger), 'and now Fournier, the taxi driver' (middle finger). 'Revenge killings?' he concluded, with a keen frown that Alain knew all too well. When laypeople start coming up with theories on criminal cases, madness usually follows.

'Probably something like that,' Alain said flatly. 'We're working on it.'

'It'll be drugs,' the mayor went on. 'Balard was a rather unsavoury character, with his nightclub. He'd been put away twice for dealing. He'll have got the others involved. The lure of profit, Inspector. Money corrupts people, turns them bad,' he uttered darkly.

'There was nothing suspicious in the notary's bank accounts, and our initial investigations haven't found anything out of the ordinary in the taxi driver's either. No stashes of cash, no strange or unexplained transactions.'

This state of apparent stalemate seemed to displease the mayor. He must have been very set on this drug theory – perhaps he was hoping for some anti-drug PR to build into his upcoming re-election campaign, railing against the scourge of our youth.

'We might be dealing with a serial killer …' Alain threw in with a smile.

The mayor looked back at him, stunned.

'Yes,' Alain went on. 'All the same victim profile, men in their fifties, and same modus operandi: victim on his knees with a bullet through his head. Always near a forest.'

'You can't be serious, Inspector,' said the mayor, his voice quavering. 'I have my citizens to think about. People are going to panic. Bourqueville is a quiet, peaceful sort of place, known for its cider and Livarot cheese, not bloody murders! The people are good, honest, hard-working folk …'

The mayor launched into a lengthy diatribe on the charm of the village, its people and the pleasures of life in the French countryside. Alain let him go on until he finally fell silent.

'I need to visit the old mayor, Jean-Paul Fournier, to inform him of his son's death. I presume you have his address.'

'Of course. I'll write it down for you. It's not easy to find – he's deep in the woods.'

He opened a drawer and took out a thick leather-bound diary, licked his thumb and flicked through the pages before taking the lid off his fountain pen. Despite the flat-screen computer and iPhone on the desk, there was something rather old-fashioned about the decor as a whole: the wood-panelled room, the photo of the President of the Republic and the white plaster bust of Marianne on the marble mantelpiece, the Empire-style desk, the glass-fronted cabinet filled with books and ornaments that hung on the wall behind the mayor's seat.

'I'll draw you a map,' said the mayor, without looking up.

Alain nodded in thanks as his eye was caught by three white shapes sitting side by side on one of the shelves in the cabinet.

'What are they?'

'What's that?' asked the mayor, glancing up from the sheet of paper.

'Those white things,' Alain said, motioning towards the shelf with his chin.

The mayor turned heavily in his chair.

'Oh, those? They're sugar flowers.'

'Sorry?'

'The great works of master patissiers. They used to sculpt them out of a block of sugar weighing several kilos, using chisels and no doubt other tools I know nothing about. Quite a feat, don't you think? The slightest mistake and the whole thing's ruined.'

Alain stood to take a closer look. The sculptures were roughly thirty centimetres tall and their bases were also carved from sugar. Each flower had a completely imaginary shape, with interwoven petals forming a delicate corolla, its thousands of crystals shimmering as if covered in morning dew. A flower plucked straight from a fairy tale.

'It was a gift to the *mairie*,' he went on, 'from a family of patissiers from Bourqueville. They had been baking and pastry-making for generations, but they're long gone. Those are the grandfather's flowers, if I'm not mistaken. The old mayor will no doubt be able to tell you more about them.'

Alain couldn't take his eyes off the flowers, brilliant white like snow in winter sun.

'What was his name, this patissier?'

'Lepage.'

An entire new neighbourhood was springing up – a new city within the city. Sophie walked alongside blocks of super-modern apartments, uninhabited, barely finished, but all long since sold off-plan. Everything was new-build in the expanded Batignolles area, which housed the new high court building, whose three stacked cubes she could make out in the distance – together they were half the height of the Eiffel Tower. The police headquarters had moved from its famous address at 36 Quai des Orfèvres on the banks of the Seine to a modern building beside the courthouse. In homage to its glorious past, it had been deemed to be number 36 on a road with no other house numbers.

'It's number 36 Nowhere Street,' joked Jérôme Baudrier, one of her police college classmates who had become an inspector and left for Paris years ago. They had stayed in touch, but only saw one another once or twice a year. A heavy-duty works vehicle went past and Sophie stepped back onto the pavement. She looked up at the balconies of one of the apartment blocks. A man was having coffee on one of them – he had even put a chair and a green plant out. All the other floors were empty. Sophie briefly wondered what life must be like for this guy, the first and, for now, the only occupant of a fifteen-storey building.

Like an enclave from the past, a small structure which had once been part of the railway station had mysteriously remained intact. Its brick walls and tiled roof emerged from a little island of green. It would surely become a hangout for future inhabitants of the area, a pick-up point for organic veg boxes or a co-working space. The road went on and on until Sophie saw a large sign with an arrow pointing towards the police headquarters.

When Violaine finally returned from her lunch break, Sophie had been waiting in her office for a good half-hour.

'I'm sorry, Inspector,' said Violaine, shaking Sophie's hand.

She seemed preoccupied, her mind on something she had no intention of sharing. Sophie was about to go on the attack about her uncooperative behaviour when Violaine opened her desk drawer and took out a cabochon ring.

'You left this behind the last time you were here.'

Sophie sometimes took the ring off when her fingers swelled up – it had always been slightly too tight – and slipped it into her pocket. It was only when she got back to Rouen that she had realised the ring was no longer on her finger nor in her pocket. She had turned the car upside down before being seized with doubt – had she even had it with her when she left for Paris? She searched the entire house and every pocket of every item of clothing, only to dissolve into tears on the sofa after an hour of looking. The ring she had feared lost for ever had suddenly reappeared in Violaine's hands, and Sophie could have hugged her. Given the context of her visit, she kept it to a simple 'Thanks very much.'

She had asked to see the diaries of every member of staff in the manuscript service, along with its director's. Since Violaine continued to insist she didn't know who the author was, the readers' room was only a starting point, and nothing was known of the author until the manuscript arrived there.

Sometimes intuition and facts seem incompatible. A cold case remains unresolved because hunches and facts cannot be reconciled. Yet dozens, hundreds of hypotheses have been considered, almost certainly including the right one. No cold case solved twenty, thirty, fifty years after the fact has brought to light a solution that had never been explored before. At some time or other, if only for a week, an afternoon or half an hour, one of the investigators must have previously discovered the truth.

She had wanted to see Jérôme for the pleasure of having coffee with him, but also to log on to Anacrim, a program which had been used to analyse criminal cases for the past fifteen years. It consisted of a digital database into which all the details of a case were entered, in order to throw up any potential flaws or inconsistencies. Tables and charts came up on-screen showing the names of suspects, accounts of their movements, pieces of evidence, timelines ... everything was taken into account by the machine, which could shed light on a detail the investigators had missed. Since the double murder which had taken place a year earlier, they had built up a whole database on the case, but the machine had thus far been unable to help them.

'I'm so sick of this view,' said Jérôme Baudrier, pointing out of his office window at the endless rows of high-rise apartment blocks and the trucks trundling constantly past. 'It feels like all the concrete on the planet is being dumped under my windows. So I put that up,' he explained, indicating the calendar pinned to the wall, with pictures of Normandy cows grazing on green meadows, 'and that's for us,' he added, showing Sophie the black-and-white photo of Georges Simenon lighting his pipe in front of the old Quai des Orfèvres.

Sophie smiled, sipping her coffee from a paper cup.

'You've still got the *drakar*.'

'That's right,' Jérôme replied, looking down at the little model of a Viking longship on his desk. He had made it himself when they were still training. It was a reproduction of a boat kept in the chateau of Robert le Diable at Moulineaux, near Rouen, on the edge of the A13 motorway. He walked around his desk, sat down and looked first at the model and then at Sophie. He drank his coffee and went quiet.

'Is everything OK, Jérôme?'

He closed his eyes and started to speak.

'The truth is, I used to be in love with you, Soph. I don't know why I'm telling you this, now's not the time and this is totally inappropriate of me, but since it's never the right time … I know you'll never get over Bruno's death, I know you can't imagine being with anybody else … but Sabine and I have broken up. And you're on your own, twiddling your thumbs in your big house, and it's the same for me in my flat, and I've been thinking about you, Soph, a lot. I don't want us to spend our lives passing each other by. So that's it, I just had to tell you. At least I've got it off my chest,' he confessed, stopping for breath.

Sophie sat staring back at him, breathing hard.

'I don't know what to say,' she finally mumbled, trying to hold back tears.

'You wanted to use Anacrim?' Jérôme went on. 'I've got something much better to show you.' He smiled.

The door looked like the entrance to a bank vault. The room was completely white and was around thirty square metres in size. The walls were covered in digital control boxes and the air was filled with a low hum. They had had to swipe their badges to get in. Jérôme had requested authorisation by phone for a 'test procedure', which had been granted. At the other end of the room stood a modern desk and a tablet computer. The screen was blue.

Jérôme told the inspector to put her hand on the tablet.

'It needs to be able to read your fingerprints.'

Sophie placed her hand on the screen. They waited.

'Hello, Inspector Tanche,' said a soothing voice, which echoed round the room. Sophie jumped and turned towards her colleague. 'I'm Anacrim 888,' the voice went on, 'I'm artificially intelligent and you can talk to me.'

'Impressive, isn't it?' exclaimed Jérôme Baudrier. 'This is for your eyes only, Soph. This room and this AI program don't officially exist. The Ministries of the Interior and Defence are trialling it here. So basically, we aren't here, we were never here.'

'Got it,' agreed Sophie. 'Can I plug in my USB?'

Sophie took out a USB stick and connected it to the computer.

'The case concerns the double murder of two joggers,' the voice said. 'And a connection with a new crime. I'd say the connection has been established. Same weapon, same method.'

'Can I really speak to it?'

'Yes, go ahead.'

'I'm not sure this is for me,' murmured Sophie, before taking a deep breath. 'There are new factors to consider.'

'What are they?' asked the voice.

'A novel which describes crimes very like those in the case. Nobody knows who wrote the book; even its editor claims to be in the dark. Everything stems from a place they call the readers' room. I want to follow this lead; I've asked all the members of staff and the director for their diaries. Christ, I'm talking to a machine,' Sophie sighed.

Baudrier placed his hand on her shoulder.

'Shh, you'll annoy it.'

'I'm not annoyed, Inspector Baudrier. People often find their first AI encounter unsettling. Coming back to your hunch about the book: we should indeed explore this avenue. What is the name of the book?'

'*Sugar Flowers*. The author's name is Camille Désencres. I've got it in my bag.'

'No need, I'll find it online. OK – I've read it.'

'You've read it?'

'Not in the same way you would read it. Let's say I've noted its contents.'

'In the space of a few seconds?'

'In a nanosecond, to be precise. The parallels with the crimes are indeed uncanny. I note one detail.'

'Go ahead.'

'The last death in the book.'

'Yes?'

'It doesn't say he has a hole in the head.'

Sophie picked up her copy of the book and reread the passage in question. The machine was right: it said he was on his knees, dead, but Camille Désencres didn't mention the weapon or the manner of injury.

'You're quite right,' she said.

'The men in the book and those in your case are very likely one and the same, Inspector.'

'My readers' room theory ... You've got all their diaries on the USB stick.'

'Yes. But your theory is highly unlikely.'

Sophie lost her cool.

'Some of them don't have an alibi!' she shot back.

'Indeed. But there's someone else involved in the case who seems a more credible fit.'

'Who?'

'Vlad Comanescu.'

Sophie turned to her colleague, who raised his eyebrows.

'He's a guy we arrested and released early on,' she told him. 'A petty criminal with links to Romanian drug traffickers. In his thirties, gun-mad.'

'His record includes convictions for various violent offences and involvement in drug trafficking,' the voice went on. 'The owner of the Thor nightclub was convicted of drug trafficking. Vlad Comanescu has just been released from prison.'

'I didn't know that,' Sophie admitted.

'He was sentenced to a year in prison for aggravated theft. His crimes have always taken place in Normandy. Technically, he's the only one to have been in the right place to commit all the crimes in this case. His previous convictions make him a prime suspect.'

Sophie was speechless on hearing this.

'You're disappointed,' Baudrier observed.

Sophie closed her eyes.

'Who wrote *Sugar Flowers*?' she asked.

'Camille Désencres,' the voice replied.

'Is there a link between my case and the book?'

'It seems there is a link, but I'm not able to trace it. I can't find the answer in the case file. I'm sorry not to be able to help, Inspector.'

The map the mayor had drawn was perfect up until the fork in the track. Alain had duly followed the arrow the mayor had drawn pointing right, but it was now obvious that the road led nowhere. It just stopped in the middle of the forest, with no clearing, just trees. He had driven around for an hour and a quarter, setting his satnav for the closest hamlet. After the robotic voice had told him all the roundabouts where he needed to take the first or second exit, or continue straight for four kilometres on the D137, the device fell silent. Alain checked the mayor's sketch once again. The arrow was definitely pointing right.

'You have arrived at your destination,' the satnav suddenly announced, making Alain jump.

'No, you fucking idiot,' he swore, 'we haven't arrived.'

'You have arrived,' the voice repeated calmly.

Alain closed his eyes and breathed in.

'You have arrived,' it went on, like a disembodied deity who was not about to be contradicted by a miserable human.

Alain undid his seat belt, got out of the car and slammed the door. He headed for the raised bank he could make out through the trees; perhaps it would give him a better view of the area. In the distance, he could see a single house. It was rather low and had a thatched roof, and someone must have been burning branches or leaves in the garden because a column of white smoke was rising skywards. Alain began to climb down the bank and cut across the fields.

When he reached the gate in the high brick wall surrounding the garden, he looked for a buzzer but found only an old bronze bell, turned green by the rain, with a cast-iron chain. This was a first, thought Alain. He knew where he was with your average doorbell or intercom, but a proper bell? He hadn't been able to forewarn the person he was going to meet by phone – nobody at the *mairie* had been able to give him a number; they imagined he probably didn't have a mobile and, if he had a landline, it was probably ex-directory. He had worked out that Jean-Paul Bouvier must be about eighty-eight. Alain cleared his throat, took two deep breaths and murmured, 'Monsieur le Maire, I'm Inspector Massard from Rouen police. I've come to give you some very bad news ...' Yeah, that sounded ok. He reached for the chain and rang the bell.

Nothing. Twice he tried, only to be greeted by silence. Alain pushed the gate open and entered the garden. Part of the plot had been turned into a vegetable patch and a statue of the Virgin Mary presided over it, perched on a rock. Did you need miracles as well as fertiliser to grow vegetables? The news Alain was bringing was not miraculous, quite the opposite, and he couldn't resist making the sign of the cross as he passed the statue. He knocked on the front door of the house and again there was no response, but the door was open and he let himself in. There was a large living space with a kitchenette which opened out onto the TV area criss-crossed with beams and containing a bar surrounded by stools. The TV was tuned to a news channel and turned up loud. Something was simmering away in a pressure cooker, which Alain guessed from the smell to be *pot-au-feu*. Moving towards the TV screen, he was confronted with the scene from that morning: the taxi – this time without the kneeling corpse – and a young woman talking into a microphone bearing her station's logo: 'There was nothing out of the ordinary about Marc Fournier, a taxi driver, yet his death has extraordinary parallels with another crime: a year ago, the bodies of notary Damien Perchaude and Sébastien Balard, who ran the Thor nightclub, were found twenty kilometres from here. Same method: bodies kneeling and a bullet through the head, and, crucially, these men knew each other. What links these three crimes? Why a year's gap before this latest murder? The police are saying little and few clues have emerged from this peaceful little village where life revolves around bowls of cider and Livarot cheese.'

The journalist had clearly spoken to the mayor and been told the usual spiel. Alain turned to the sofa and jumped. An elderly man was sitting perfectly still, propped up on three cushions, staring at Alain like an aged bird of prey.

'I'm Inspector Massard from Rouen police,' Alain introduced himself. 'I came to inform you of your son's death, but I can see you already know about it …'

The old man turned off the television and looked down at the floor, shaking his head.

'Monsieur le Maire, what's going on? Why are they all dying?'

The former official looked Alain straight in the eye.

'Talk to me …' Alain went on gently. 'What did they do wrong? You know – I'm sure you do,' he pushed him.

The old man went on staring at him, mouth closed.

They sat watching one another for some time. Alain knew them well, these villagers who kept their lips firmly sealed and steadfastly refused to give away the slightest hint about a family secret or suspicious death. You could inflict all the tortures of the Middle Ages on them and still they would keep everything they knew to themselves.

'Patissier Lepage's sugar flowers, they're the key to this, aren't they? The Lepage name?'

The man remained silent.

'You don't want to talk to me … you're never going to talk!' Alain fumed.

He took his phone out of his pocket and did a Google images search for 'Violaine Lepage'. He clicked on her official picture on the publisher's website, which showed Violaine against a black background, surrounded by piles of books. He enlarged it to full screen and waved it under the ex-mayor's nose.

'Do you know this woman?'

The old man looked at the photo, closed his eyes and turned away. Alain calmed down. Getting angry with a man old enough to be his grandfather, and, who, in addition, had just heard his son had died, suddenly seemed as pointless as it was inappropriate. Contrary to all expectations, the old man raised his hand as if in surrender, and Alain thought for a moment he was going to talk. But, as if he were mute, he signalled to Alain to stay on the sofa while he heaved himself to his feet and headed over to the kitchen. He turned off the gas under the *pot-au-feu*, walked over to the stairs and began to climb, until he disappeared from sight.

Alain imagined he must be going to look for something. But what? A metal box filled with yellowed photographs? Would he then start to talk? It occurred to him he might instead have gone to fetch a rifle with which to shoot Alain from the top of the stairs before turning the gun on himself. Alain felt for his weapon and released the safety catch. The room and the house had been quiet for several minutes. He looked towards the kitchen window; a wasp was trying to get in. He heard a low thud and looked up at the ceiling. It sounded like something falling over, a lamp or an ashtray.

'Monsieur le Maire?' he called up. 'Monsieur Fournier?'

Alain stood up and started up the stairs. The revolver in his hand felt unnecessary but somehow reassuring. When he reached the first floor, he repeated, 'Monsieur?' A door stood ajar; he pushed it open. The old man was swaying gently from the end of a rope tied around a cross-beam, a stool lying on the ground next to him. Alain stood stunned for a moment before racing downstairs to the kitchen to find a knife. He ran back up, scrambled onto the stool and started cutting the thin rope which refused to give way until the last strand of nylon. The ex-mayor's body fell with all its weight, knocking Alain and the stool over with it. Turning painfully onto his side, Alain saw that the man's eyes were open, his head resting against the floor.

'I'm a monster …'

'No, you have a complex personality,' Stein countered, taking a drag on his e-cigarette.

The psychoanalyst's office was in semi-darkness with the curtains drawn, as usual, but it seemed to Violaine as if the subtle lighting was even dimmer than normal. She could barely make Stein out through the thick puff of smoke from his new vaping device.

'I love Édouard, only him, and I'm cheating on him. Why would I do that?'

The only reply was the sizzling sound of the cigarette.

'You're not saying anything, Pierre. Speak, damn you …'

They had just been talking about Violaine's lovers, a list of whom Stein claimed to have compiled from her confessions. He had refused to give her the names.

'You'll either find them in your subconscious, or you won't. It doesn't really matter. It'll come back to you in flashbacks, like random shots from a porn film.'

In reply, Violaine had thrown a cushion from the couch at Pierre, which he caught in mid-air and slipped behind his back.

'I've had enough of this couch.'

Violaine stood up, leaning on her cane.

'Rebellion ...' said Stein, studying her with interest.

'Maybe,' she replied, walking over to a set of shelves filled with terracotta pots, jugs and dishes. 'Why do you collect this kind of pottery? You have no connection to the countryside. I doubt you've seen a cow in your life.'

Pierre smiled.

'It's a collection when you have two and are looking for a third,' he declared.

'Like me and my lovers?'

Once again, all she got back was a hissing sound followed by a cloud of smoke.

'"I know those two men" – that's what you said about the two who were killed in the same way as the characters in *Sugar Flowers*.'

'Another man has been killed ...'

'Do you think you know him too?'

Violaine didn't reply.

'Silence is an answer,' Stein remarked tersely. 'Why didn't you have children?' he suddenly went on.

'I can't have them.'

'You can't or you won't?'

'Can't and won't. I don't want to be separated from the man I love by anything or anyone. I want to stay just the two of us, not three, four, five of us. Two of us, always! Is that a good enough answer for you?'

'It's an answer ...' Stein said softly.

Violaine went up to the mantelpiece and looked in the mirror.

'I gave Inspector Tanche her ring back. I stole it off her.'

'Good,' Stein said approvingly, in another puff of vape smoke.

'And I saw Proust in the Jardin du Luxembourg. Doesn't that surprise you?' she said, turning to him.

'You're changing the subject. Go on, then, let's talk about

Proust. You saw him, and then what? It's an emotional projection.'

'I spoke to him, Pierre, and he replied,' Violaine insisted, lying back on the couch.

'That doesn't worry me,' Stein shot back, blowing smoke towards the ceiling. 'I had a patient who had been speaking to his dead Labrador for over twenty years. There was nothing eccentric about him – he was chief exec of a CAC 40 company. At difficult moments in his life, he saw the dog at his side. It reassured him. Did it reassure you, seeing Proust?'

'Yes.'

'Maybe he really was with you. We don't know very much about what happens after death. The answers offered by religion are either far too precise or far too vague. Neither will do.'

'You're not taking me seriously.'

'No, I'm deadly serious. Is there anything else?'

Violaine brought her leg back up onto the couch and stroked the metal rods, staring up at the ceiling.

'Pierre, could I have written *Sugar Flowers* and not remember it?'

'… Would you like to have written it?'

'Yes,' Violaine whispered.

'Why?'

Violaine said nothing more. The hiss of the cigarette was the only sound to be heard until the end of the session.

The firemen had taken away the body and a neighbour had given the phone number of a woman who lived thirty kilometres away who was to be called 'in an emergency'. Alain found himself returning to his stock phrases: 'Something very serious has happened to the former mayor.' This time, he had kept things simple, following up with: 'He chose to end his own life very suddenly.' The woman simply replied, 'I'm on my way,' and Alain explained, 'I'll be gone by the time you arrive, Madame, I need to vacate the premises. I'll give you the number for the chief fire officer.'

He felt completely empty and felt no shame in sitting at the kitchen counter, pouring himself a large glass of red wine and drinking it in front of the firemen. Then he took a call from Sophie asking him to immediately follow up the lead – abandoned a year earlier – on Vlad Comanescu. Their discussion had been so heated that the firemen had twice turned to look at him while they were zipping the old man into a body bag and lifting him onto a stretcher. Voices had been raised.

'No!' Alain protested. 'The old man didn't go and hang himself because his son was involved in drugs! He refused to reply when I asked him about the sugar flowers. He wouldn't say a word about the Lepage patissiers. He looked away when I showed him the picture of your editor. He hanged himself out of shame, Sophie, and to avoid having to talk. I saw the sugar flowers – I saw them with my own eyes!'

Nevertheless he had put out an urgent search warrant for Vlad Comanescu before getting into his car, unplugging the satnav and speeding back towards Rouen.

Inside the huge archive room of the *mairie*, Alain was now sitting at a little desk, sorting files by name and profession and cross-referencing them. Though many archives had been digitised, those of Rouen's *boulangers-pâtissiers* were not among them. All kinds of information about the present day was accessible on the internet and intranet, along with plenty of detail on the distant past, especially if it was likely to be of interest to tourists. Yet the life of Rouen's shopkeepers who had come and gone more or less unnoticed did not figure in the department's grand plans for digitalisation. Thus Alain was forced to leaf through yellowed records of businesses, births and deaths.

An hour later, he tracked down Boulangerie-Pâtisserie Lepage. Opened twenty-five years ago. Later sold. He found what he was looking for in the registers of births and deaths.

His black Moleskine notebook contained two full pages of crossings out before this summary appeared:

'Originally from Bourqueville, Henri and Pauline Lepage. Henri, artisan patissier, and Pauline, midwife, and their children, Hélène and Fabienne. Fabienne was born eighteen years after Hélène, and died a year ago.'

The record he had found indicated that Fabienne had committed suicide by jumping from a window. Her parents had died in a car accident a few months previously. Hélène, on the other hand, seemed to have vanished into thin air. There was no mention of a Violaine Lepage.

'Why so long between the births of the two children? Why did the second daughter kill herself?' Alain noted. He also noticed that Hélène's date of birth corresponded to the editor's age and wrote down one last question: 'Are Hélène and Violaine the same person?'

He sensed he was finally getting to the bottom of the case. Sophie could get lost with her AI program, and Vlad Comanescu could go on with his small-time drug deals. Alain had the vague, exhilarating feeling he was getting closer to the truth – he could almost touch it. The sugar flowers in the cabinet in the mayor's office in Bourqueville, that name – Lepage – that kept coming up, the old man who had hanged himself rather than say what he knew … All these pieces were surely falling into place. And it had nothing whatsoever to do with drugs or the dodgy associates of the man who ran Thor. The answer lay much further back. The solution was in the past. It was also based on Sophie's hunch that everything stemmed from the readers' room. Alain closed his eyes and tried to clear his mind in order to bring all the elements together. If he could do that, a theory would jump out, a theory that would strike like lightning, and the truth would burst forth. He groped around for it, like someone waking up in a dark room in the middle of the night, feeling for the door handle and heading to the kitchen to find water. He could sense that the source was near. It was beginning to come together; Sophie was right, everything stemmed from the readers' room … In less than a minute, he would come up with a credible hypothesis … His telephone, on vibrate, suddenly made him jump. He picked up the phone to one of his colleagues.

'Alain,' the caller began, 'we've just knocked down a stud wall in the taxi driver's cellar. There are crates and crates of ecstasy and coke – they must be worth millions! … Can you hear me?' he asked, when Alain said nothing.

'Yes, I can hear you,' he managed to reply. Then he hung up.

Alain looked down at the registers spread around him and his notebook, dazed. Everything had gone up in flames. There were no cards left on the table. The game was over – it had never begun. He closed all the registers, put them back on the shelves, slipped his notebook into his pocket and left.

The bright white sky and the sound of passing cars was so overwhelming that he took out his dark glasses. Just an average case of score-settling and drugs … He walked a few hundred metres, his mind empty, before finding himself outside the church of Saint-Laurent, which housed the Musée Le Secq des Tournelles. Alain was overcome with a feeling of weariness. The desire to see Virginie, to sleep with her – or maybe even not – crossed his mind. He sat down on the steps of the church. What stood out about this museum was its collections of keys: hundreds of them, finely wrought and lined up in glass cases. No one would ever know what doors they were designed to open, and where these doors led: into drawing rooms, bedrooms, gardens? You'd have to be mad to collect keys to who knew what. Unless it wasn't the door that mattered, but having the key. Then Alain realised he was talking to himself.

A few days later, Rouen regional crime squad arrested Vlad Comanescu during a stake-out in Le Grand-Quevilly. He quickly confessed: he had indeed been sent to kill the nightclub owner, his notary friend and the taxi driver by the head of a Romanian gang. The owner of Thor had pretended the drugs he was hiding for them had been stolen so that he could sell them himself and keep the profits, helped by two friends who had each been promised a cut. A few days after the double murder, Vlad had been arrested for aggravated theft. He was a repeat offender on a suspended sentence; he was immediately brought before a court and sent down for a year. Upon his release, he fulfilled the last part of the contract in order to get his hands on the money he had been promised for the three executions.

Among his possessions were thirty thousand euros in cash and the Luger P08 which was identified as the murder weapon. He had bought it on the black market for old weapons. A pistol which had been out of circulation since the war had seemed a wise choice.

As she left the station where he had been remanded in custody, Sophie booked a day's leave for the date the Prix Goncourt would be awarded, before heading home to bed.

PART III

There were reporters' cars parked on Place Gaillon, a satellite dish had been unloaded from a van, and a police car with four sergeants inside was parked in front of the famous restaurant – they would escort the winner to the entrance when the crowds got too big. The literary world was starting to flock to Drouant. The restaurant was carefully checking the credentials of those passing through its entrance to gather on the ground floor. Outside, an Italian television crew was interviewing passers-by, probably asking them about what they liked reading and whether they would buy the winning book. Journalists with press cards and editors who were so well-known they didn't need a pass, were now steadily streaming past and were given fabric wristbands with 'Prix Goncourt' printed on them, allowing them to come and go as they pleased. A private terrace had been set up and small groups were starting to gather there, while others shook hands or exchanged kisses. A secret, powerful miniature world was coming together again for a celebration full of suspense.

Sophie, squeezed into her leather biker jacket, was smoking and watching from across the road. She spotted a few famous journalists and was almost tempted to have a look inside so she could listen to conversations and see everything up close – predictions, reviews and rumours must have been making the rounds. A police ID card was still the best way in, and just imagining the face of the pretty but disagreeable girl on the door when she showed her crime squad ID made her smile. Violaine and her team must have been together at the office. Sophie looked at her watch before heading for the metro.

She did not have to show her card at the publishing house. The girl at the front desk immediately informed her that 'Madame Lepage' was in her office – her two previous visits had not gone unnoticed, thought Sophie. All the members of the manuscript service were in their large office on the first floor, but they didn't seem to be reading. Murielle, Marie and Stéphane looked at her and nodded in greeting, continuing to watch her as she headed for Violaine's door. She had asked them what they were doing on the days of the crimes – the double murder of the previous year and the more recent one. Perhaps they held it against her? Or perhaps not. Sometimes suspects who have been cleared are not actually that aggrieved: they feel as if they have been part of something out of the ordinary and will have a story to tell for the rest of their lives.

Violaine's office gave onto a large room, where her assistant was. There was also a large sofa and reclining comfortably upon it was a man who looked strangely like Serge Gainsbourg, if it weren't for the fact that he was wearing a black three-piece suit instead of the singer's customary jeans. He looked up just as she stopped in front of him.

'Pierre Stein.'

'Sophie Tanche.'

'It's you … Don't forget your ring this time,' he added. 'Violaine told me about that. I'm her psychoanalyst and friend. She tells me almost everything – though not quite everything.'

Stein made her feel oddly both comfortable and uneasy.

'Can you feel the tension? They're waiting for the results,

terrified at the idea of losing and perhaps even more of winning. It's like the smell of gas before everything blows up.'

Actually, he reminded her of the Cheshire Cat in *Alice in Wonderland*, sitting on his branch, smiling calmly and mischievously. The one who observes everything that is going on and works out what will happen next, but doesn't reveal it.

'I can feel it,' Sophie replied.

'Who will strike the match?' asked Stein, cryptically. 'You, perhaps?'

Sophie said nothing, and her eyes fell upon a man with short brown hair wearing a white shirt, who was standing in front of a window.

'Who's that?' she asked Stein.

'Édouard, her husband ... If he's around, Violaine can't be far away.' Stein took a drag on his e-cigarette. 'They are the strongest couple I've ever seen,' he added. 'A textbook example of a happy marriage.' And he exhaled a cloud of white vapour. Violaine appeared in the doorway of her office, leaning on her cane, and she met Sophie's eye.

When Pascal had called her in to tell her it was time to send for Camille Désencres, she had remained silent for a long while before admitting that just two hours before the results were announced, she did not know the identity of the author of *Sugar Flowers*. Pascal's face fell.

'Are you joking?' he had asked, flatly.

'No.'

'But a week ago you told me ... You even said she was a woman!'

'I told you what you wanted to hear. I lied to you, I'm sorry.'

'I don't know what to say.'

'Me neither.'

And Violaine stood up. Since then, nobody had seen Pascal, who had shut himself away in his office, while Violaine was in hers.

The light was streaming in through the yellow silk from Lyon patterned with scrolls and birds. Édouard had been right to choose that fabric, mused Sophie, thinking to herself that it was the last time she would enter this office, whose decor was in fact more like that of an apartment.

'I was wrong,' began Sophie; 'it was all linked to drugs. I wanted to tell you and apologise for having bothered you all – you and your manuscript service. I've brought you a note about the outcome of the investigation.'

Violaine nodded but didn't seem to have heard her. She was standing up, leaning on her cane, outlined against the window.

'Contrails ...'

'Sorry?'

'Contrails, that's what you call the white streaks aeroplanes leave in the sky. It seems like they'll be there for ever, but then they fade and nothing is left behind.'

Sophie went over to the window to look at the long white lines intersecting one another in the blue sky.

'Why did you think it all started here?' asked Violaine, without taking her eyes off the sky.

'A hunch. I think Simenon's days are over, Madame Lepage; I solved my case with artificial intelligence.'

'You haven't solved anything, Inspector,' muttered Violaine. 'Simenon is still a genius and if we win this prize, it'll be the end of my career.'

Sophie wanted to say something comforting, but she couldn't think of anything. She turned to the window: in the blue sky, the vapour trails were already starting to fade, and she thought of Jérôme Baudrier at '36 Nowhere Street'. Perhaps he was right, perhaps they shouldn't spend their whole lives missing one another – and, for the first time in many years, she felt something beating where her heart was.

'Stay and have coffee,' Violaine offered. 'I'll see you in the readers' room.'

Once the inspector had gone, Violaine stared at the dark screen of her mobile phone. The only person she would have wanted to call was Charles. She opened one of the drawers of her desk and got out the tennis ball she had taken from the court on the day he collapsed, placed her fingers on top of it, closed her eyes and whispered, 'Charles, help me, I beg you. I'm lost ...' Violaine let the ball roll along her desk and bounce across the floor until it came to a stop in a corner of the room, then she took her phone and left, leaning on her cane. Édouard and Stein had been talking outside her door and fell into step behind her, when the name 'Béatrice' came up on her mobile.

'I know what you're going to ask, Béatrice,' she announced wearily. 'No, the author isn't here, and I am committing professional suicide.'

'No,' said Béatrice, 'that's impossible. I can't believe she won't come.'

'She, he … we'll never know,' Violaine concluded as she went towards the readers' room.

Béatrice said nothing for a second, and then, emphatically: 'It is a "she".'

'How can you be sure of that?' Violaine's expression changed. 'Wait, you wrote the reader's report … Béatrice, you know who it is,' said Violaine, coming to a halt at the doorway of the readers' room, where Murielle, Marie, Stéphane and Inspector Tanche were drinking coffee.

'I promised her I wouldn't say anything about our meeting, but I'm breaking our pact; it's all got too serious now. Someone came to see me. It was just after the book was printed. She rang at my door and introduced herself as Camille Désencres. She said she wanted to see me because I had read her book and written that it should be published. I was alone with her … I'm sorry, I can't tell you what she looked like, I didn't feel her face. From her footsteps on my wooden floorboards, I'd say she weighs about fifty kilos. Her voice was that of someone around twenty-five to thirty; she doesn't speak very much; she's shy; she wears soft ballet pumps, and her perfume … I remember her perfume, it's that white, slightly powdery flower …'

'Jasmine …' whispered Violaine.

'Yes, that's it, jasmine.'

Violaine slowly turned to Marie.

'Marie … *you* wrote *Sugar Flowers*.' Marie looked at Violaine, and everyone in the readers' room looked at Marie, including Sophie who remained motionless, contemplating the young blonde woman with the pale eyes who seemed just as determined as she was scared. She hadn't been wrong: it had all started in this room.

'But … who are you, Marie?' asked Violaine.

Marie carried on looking at her, saying nothing. Then, all in one breath, she said, 'And you … who are you, Violaine?'

Violaine remained silent.

They looked at one another. It was like a scene from a waxwork museum, where life-size figures are frozen in a single action and place supposed to represent the very essence of their lives. She stopped blinking her green eyes and seemed no longer to see Marie, just as Marie now seemed lost in memories that only she knew.

'They are creatures from a book,' whispered Stein; 'they cannot speak.'

Sophie looked at Stein, who bowed his head as if assenting to a proposition that Sophie hadn't yet put into words.

'Bring me some paper and two pens,' said Sophie suddenly. Murielle did as she was told. She placed some blank sheets on two desks facing one another and put a pen on top of the paper.

'Now, everyone out,' ordered Sophie. 'You too, Monsieur Lavour. You, stay here,' she said to Stein. And she closed the door. 'We'll start with "My name is",' she said, before turning to Stein, who nodded in approval.

Marie and Violaine each looked at their white piece of paper, as if it were a puddle of water in which their faces would be reflected. They both appeared to be holding their breath. Stein didn't take his eyes off Violaine, whose vein was throbbing in her neck. There was something fascinating about the stillness of her body. Even Inspector Tanche leant against the shelves, completely motionless.

She was thinking to herself that in a room where people read words written by others, other words were now going to be written for the first time, right before her eyes. The most important words of an entire lifetime. Marie's breathing became louder, and then weaker. There were a few moments of hesitation, during which Sophie cast a worried look at Stein, who blinked in response – a sign that he still had faith. They were both going to open up; it wasn't crazy to ask them to write it down. The last second seemed to go on for a long time in deathly silence.

Violaine was the first to do something, abrupt and determined: she took the lid off her pen with a metallic clink and put pen to paper; Marie immediately followed suit. Like two soldiers drawing their swords for a duel, they began to write.

My name is Violaine Lepage; my real name is Hélène Lepage.

I was born in Normandy in a village called Bourqueville. I am the daughter of an artisan patissier and a midwife. I was not destined to enter the world of literature or become an editor. Writing these words is driving me crazy; I am going to reveal things I have never told my husband. Things I have never told my therapist. Things I have never told anyone.

Twenty-five years ago, I was someone else. A young woman who had just taken her baccalaureate and didn't like reading that much, who dreamed of boys and freedom. Thor changed my life. It had been a nice day; I should have been happy with the sun and not gone out that night. I've been terrified of the night ever since. As soon as the sun sets, I am frightened. I shouldn't have been allowed to leave. But I left. To dance and have fun – or pretend to.

I went on my moped and met some 'friends' there, whose names I now couldn't tell you. Later in the night, I met the inseparable gang of four: Sébastien Balard, son of the owner of Thor; Damien Perchaude, the notary's son; Marc Fournier, the mayor's son; and Pierre Lacaze. It was the summer after our baccalaureate. We had all passed apart from Lacaze, who said he didn't give a damn, he was going to be a master chef and didn't need maths and literature for that.

I remember the music, I remember the bar. Thor was outside

Bourqueville, near the forest. They bought me drinks. Did they put something in them? I've often asked myself. I'll never know.

I remember that we left the club to go and smoke with other people; I remember the four of them being around me. There was a strange atmosphere. I think they'd taken stuff. Sébastien Balard did pot and coke, he also took ecstasy. I should have sensed the danger. It was obvious. They suggested going for a walk to the edge of the forest. I went with them and, at some point, realised that I was the only one left; the people who had been hanging around the group hadn't come with us. Marc Fournier wanted to kiss me, and I said no. He was insistent. I said no again, and Balard grabbed me by the wrists while Perchaude lifted me off the ground, holding me by the hips. I remember shouting. I remember my panic. After that, I don't remember anything.

After that, it gets too violent and I won't be able to write it down. I know I wake up in Lacaze's car and they take me home. They seem annoyed. I go in via the gate at the end of the farm and I think: I was raped, they raped me. I refuse to believe it, and yet I have images in my head and I can still feel them inside me; I know they hold me by the hands, I know that I shout. I saw condoms being passed around. I still refuse to believe it happened. The next day, my parents ask me if I had a good time and I say yes. When I realise my periods have stopped, I put it down to nervous shock and I carry on that way for a long time. Too long. Nowadays it's called denial of pregnancy, but I'd never heard that expression at the time. I am slim and I don't put on any weight, then I have doubts. I'm going to go back to study humanities. I go to see a doctor and he tells me I'm pregnant. He's not especially surprised that I'm still not showing; he tells me that that happens sometimes, but that it won't take me long to start showing. I ask him if I can have an abortion and his eyes widen. 'It's too late. Even abroad,' he adds. 'But ... what happened to you, mademoiselle?' I think it struck him that it was serious, but I said nothing and left without paying. Running. At that moment, I decide something: I am going to kill myself. There's a *weapon in the cellar – the SS pistol that my grandfather found when the Germans fled after the Normandy landings. It's in its box, with the bullets. I'll load it, turn it on myself and shoot.*

My father caught me. It was a Sunday. I had to tell my parents everything, absolutely everything. My father went mad; he took the pistol and left, saying that he would kill all of them. We didn't see him until evening. He came back and he hadn't killed anyone. I was angry with him, I hated him. I stopped loving him. My mother decided to calm things down: she sent my father to bed and took me aside. She told me I had no other choice but to carry the pregnancy to term. I said I would kill myself first. To her, children were sacred and the idea that some women gave them up to social services was sickening.

So, she offered me a deal to make sure I stayed alive: I would have the child and, since I couldn't stand the idea of seeing it or raising it, she would say it was hers and raise it herself. I wouldn't even have to say that I had ever been pregnant. I would give birth at home. She would register it as her own and nobody would ever be able to check.

I realised that for my whole life, I would have a brother or sister who would in fact be my son or daughter, and I hated my mother.

The birth of that child meant leaving my family for ever; I would never see them again. I would be replaced by that child. I had organised my own replacement. I had killed Hélène Lepage.

I looked at my parents and all I could see was a coward and a madwoman.

I lived like a hermit until I gave birth. I didn't do my first year of university. I lived in bed and all I did was read – all the French classics, with a particular liking for Marcel Proust. I read tens, hundreds of books. I also read Modiano, Echenoz, Murakami and Stephen King, all the authors I would one day know in person. I made my parents go and buy me their novels or look for them in the library.

I'm not going to talk about giving birth, alone with my mother. I know they called her Fabienne.

Afterwards, we left for Rouen and parted ways. My mother registered the child as her own at the town hall, claiming she had given birth at home. I lived off odd jobs and went to uni. And I found a job at a bookshop. I didn't have any money. At the time, I would often sleep with people for money. I don't know how many times. I was a bookseller part-time and I would sleep with men in the evenings, arranging meetings on the phone, but I wasn't coping and felt my life was imploding around me. Then, one day, I was finally able to leave. For Paris.

I met Charles. Then Édouard. They are the only men who have ever meant anything to me.

I decided to rename myself Violaine after the heroine in a Paul Claudel text I read during my reclusive days, but I did it mostly because the first four letters of the new name were a statement of my violation. Hélène's life may have ended one night on the way out of a club, but Violaine would go as far as you can possibly go.

When I read Sugar Flowers, *I realised straight away that the author knew about my past. The men who raped me were immediately recognisable. Someone had written about what I wanted to do: kill all of them. And had written about it better than I ever could. I was stunned. And panicked.*

At the publishing house, everybody gave the text, and the writing, the green light – even Béatrice. Backing out was impossible; I had to publish it. The author was still nowhere to be seen. And I have these gaps in my memory too, so in the end I gave up on looking and even understanding. I let fate take its course, and it has brought me here today to reveal everything about myself, in the room that is my whole life. This is where the path leads: it was written in the stars, as they say.

My father sold the Luger when we left for Rouen. The weapon used in the crimes in Sugar Flowers *is a similar model – or maybe it's the same one, maybe it never left the area and has re-emerged twenty-five years later … The one I once held in my hands.*

In investigating one case, Inspector Tanche has unearthed another. I think I had been waiting a long time for somebody to set me free or release me.

Now I want to tell my story to the man who is my whole life, the man who loves me and whom I have loved for so many years, and who doesn't know about my past: Édouard, my husband. Let me share this with him.

But first, I'll let you read these pages.

Here you go, Marie, and I'll read yours too.

The inspector will read my story and so will Stein.

Everyone will know everything.

The reading panel will be closed.

Then this will just be between Édouard and me.

Violaine Lepage

My name is Marie Cassart and I was Fabienne Lepage's girlfriend. She was the love of my life. We met at college; we both knew we liked girls and were inseparable. Fabienne ended her life a year ago. Her parents had died in a car accident a few months before. Fabienne found out that they were in fact her grandparents and had had a daughter before her: Hélène Lepage. They had never mentioned her.

She found everything out in the family record book when she was registering their deaths. At first, Fabienne thought she had a sister. She got out her mother's private diaries. We spent an entire weekend reading them, travelling back in time to find out what happened twenty-five years earlier. Her mother had written it all down, along with everyone's names.

Hélène had gone to a nightclub and run into the sons of the great and the good of Bourqueville, who had been drinking or taking drugs. They led her into the forest and took turns raping her.

She didn't say anything when she got home. Then one day, her father found her in the cellar with the pistol left behind by the SS division that had occupied Bourqueville during the war. She wanted to kill herself. He managed to stop her and she revealed everything — the rape and the pregnancy, and that it was too late for a legal abortion. Her father took the gun. He went to see the mayor of Bourqueville and his son denied it; the mayor threatened him and told him he didn't have any proof. He went to see the notary and was told the same thing. The owner of Thor threw him out, as did Pierre Lacaze's father.

When he got back, he realised he had turned the whole village against him. The situation was unbearable. He decided to move to Rouen.

Meanwhile, the women had been talking. Hélène's mother had offered her a deal: stay at home while you are pregnant. Don't let anyone see you. Until they moved to Rouen. Her daughter would give birth at home and she would register the child as her own.

Hélène agreed, on the condition that she would never see the child and would never see her parents again.

The diary from those nine months didn't say much, other than that Hélène was always reading books, novels, and Proust especially. You could tell that she was hard on her parents.

Her father managed to sell his bakery and find an apartment, as well as another shop to buy in Rouen. He sold the family farm buildings and they left as soon as the child was born. They named her Fabienne. She wasn't born at hospital, so nobody at the town hall asked any questions.

Hélène left them and found herself a little studio in the old part of Rouen. They never saw each other again. They would sometimes bump into each other in the street, the child in her pushchair. Hélène would turn away and, one day, she disappeared completely.

You have to skip years of the diary to find her again. Hélène's mother writes that she sees her on a literary programme on television one evening. She is an editor and goes by the name of Violaine Lepage.

Fabienne spent the whole weekend drunk. Then she sobered up at the beginning of the week. She seemed strangely calm; she told me she wanted to write a book telling this story, in which the narrator would kill the four men who had raped her real mother, one after the other. A bullet to the head, kneeling down, with the SS Luger mentioned in the diary. She would send the text to Violaine and she would understand.

She didn't want to turn up empty-handed, but armed with the truth, and this truth had to be in the form of a novel. She would say it all the time: not turning up empty-handed. The novel would be called Sugar Flowers, *like the ones her grandfather had crafted out of sugar loaf.*

She found them all, tracking them down on the internet: the notary's son who had taken over the family practice, the owner of Thor who had taken over the club from his father, the mayor's son who had become a taxi driver and chef Pierre Lacaze who had taken off for Los Angeles. Fabienne had lost her mind, but I didn't realise.

One day she told me she was going to start writing. The next day, she threw herself out of the window of our apartment. She didn't leave anything behind — not a word, not a letter. Just the computer screen with the title, Sugar Flowers, *written on it.*

On the day of her funeral, the men she had wanted to kill in her book made the front pages: the owner of Thor and the notary had been killed, kneeling down, with bullets to their heads. They died just as she had imagined they would. That was a year ago.

It was like Fabienne was giving me a sign from the afterlife.

Reality had been twisted into the book she wanted to write. I decided to write this book so Fabienne would remain with me. I told myself that reality might carry on matching up to her imaginings, eventually leading her to Violaine.

I know now that that's what happened.

The men are all dying in the same way as in the book. I don't know why, but that's how it is.

The book is living its own life.

All books are works of black magic.

I came to Paris to finish my thesis. Meeting Violaine had become an obsession. I was writing Sugar Flowers *and would keep watch outside the publishing house. The first time I saw her leaving, my heart started racing and I felt like I was paralysed. One evening, I followed her. She stopped outside the door of a building and I saw the Alcoholics*

Anonymous symbol on a little sign. She lit a cigarette, seeming to hesitate. I stayed close to her, watching with fascination. I had finished Sugar Flowers just the night before – everything coincided. She turned round and looked at me. I must have seemed hesitant. 'I guess you're going to the same place as me?' she asked. I said yes. 'Well, I'm not going, I've changed my mind.' I told her I was thinking the same thing. She suggested that I join her, and we go for a walk.

Night had started to fall and I walked through the streets beside her; it was like a dream. I thought about Fabienne. I told her that I had lost the love of my life and that she was a girl. It didn't seem to shock her and she listened for a long time. We went on walking. I told her about my thesis on objects in literature. We bumped into Modiano on a street corner and Violaine called him by his first name. We ended up at the publishing house. It was dark. Violaine said: 'Well, we're not such anonymous alcoholics any more – do you want a drink? I've got an excellent whisky.'

We found ourselves in this empty room, her office, looking at one another and drinking whisky. At one point I wondered if she was hitting on me, but no, it wasn't like that – she was observing me, with her green eyes and sphinx-like air. It was surreal. I had a feeling we had come to the end of our journey. Violaine lit a cigarette, exhaled and asked me a question: 'Do you know what a manuscript service is?'

She also gave me the card of her therapist, Pierre Stein. She told me he might be able to help me with the loss of my friend. She was incredibly kind. Everyone said she was harsh and scheming, but it's not true – she is one of the most sensitive women I've ever met. I love her. I'd like her to be my sister, my friend, my lover, my mother. The next day, Violaine called me in to give me some manuscripts, and I joined the department as Fleur's replacement.

Pierre Stein was the first to read Sugar Flowers. I told him everything. He insisted that Violaine had to read the book. It was his idea for me to send it to the manuscript service, embellished with the sun that I drew on it. We would then let fate take its course. Then Béatrice voted for it and so did the reading panel, and it all got out of control. We invented Camille Désencres, with only an email address for contact. It was Stein who signed the contract from London, where he was staying for a conference. Sometimes he replied to emails, sometimes I did. Then the book got swept up in all the madness of the Prix Goncourt …

Camille Désencres does not exist. She is Fabienne, me, Stein and Violaine.

Marie Cassart

At eight minutes past midday, the Prix Goncourt was awarded to *Our Empty Childhoods* by Bruno Tardier. *Sugar Flowers* missed out by two votes in the tenth round.

Édouard and Violaine talked until nightfall and then they went to bed. Violaine pressed herself up against Édouard until their bodies became one. He could feel her breath in his ear. 'Don't say anything, I know what you're thinking,' he murmured. 'You're thinking, "You must never let me go away." I never will.'

He pulled her even closer and put his lips to her neck to breathe in the fragrance of her hair and her skin, thinking that he could never do without her and had never loved her so much; that life did not exist without Violaine Lepage, Head of Manuscript Services. The woman whose secrets he now knew.

That evening at a restaurant called Le Louis XIX, Pierre Lacaze, the last of the four men who had taken Violaine into the forest, felt the first signs of a heart attack, sweating coupled with a shooting pain in his left arm and the sensation that his chest was being ripped apart from inside. He left the kitchen and his twelve commis chefs, and rushed up to his office to look for his glyceryl trinitrate spray and call an ambulance. They think he felt faint before he could take the medicine and make the phone call. They found him kneeling, head tilted forward, in front of the big poster of Los Angeles at night that adorned his wall.

> Kneeling before the big city, his soul will have been carried away in the river of red and yellow car lights. It will be sucked in and wiped away.
>
> The time for vengeance is now over, as all debts have been paid.
>
> Our love can now at last begin in happiness.

Thus ended *Sugar Flowers*.

Vintage 1954
Antoine Laurain

Translated by Jane Aitken & Emily Boyce

'A glorious time-slip caper . . . Just wonderful' *Daily Mail*

'Delightfully nostalgic escapism set in a gorgeously conjured Paris of 1954' *Sunday Mirror*

When Hubert Larnaudie invites some fellow residents of his Parisian apartment building to drink an exceptional bottle of 1954 Beaujolais, he has no idea of its special properties. The following morning, Hubert finds himself waking up in 1950s Paris, as do antique restorer Magalie, mixologist Julien, and Airbnb tenant Bob from Milwaukee, who's on his first trip to Europe.

After their initial shock, the city of Edith Piaf and *An American in Paris* begins to work its charm on them. The four delight in getting to know the French capital during this iconic period, whilst also playing with the possibilities that time travel allows. But, ultimately, they need to work out how to get back to 2017. And the key lies in a legendary story and the vineyards of the Chateau St Antoine . . .

ISBN: 9781910477670
e-ISBN: 9781910477694

Smoking Kills
Antoine Laurain

Translated by Louise Rogers Lalaurie

'Funny, superbly over-the-top . . . not a page too much'
The Times

'Hilarious . . . formidable – and essential packing for any French
summer holiday' *Daily Mail*

When head-hunter Fabrice Valentine faces a smoking ban at
work, he decides to undertake a course of hypnotherapy to rid
himself of the habit. At first the treatment works, but his stress
levels begin to rise when he is passed over for an important
promotion and he finds himself lighting up again – but with none
of his previous enjoyment.

Until he discovers something terrible: he accidentally causes a
man's death, and needing a cigarette to calm his nerves, he enjoys
it more than any other previous smoke. What if he now needs to
kill every time he wants to properly appreciate his next Benson
and Hedges?

ISBN: 9781910477540
e-ISBN: 9781910477557

The Red Notebook
Antoine Laurain

Translated by Jane Aitken & Emily Boyce

'A clever, funny novel . . . a masterpiece of Parisian perfection'
HRH The Duchess of Cornwall

'Resist this novel if you can; it's the very quintessence of French
romance' *The Times*

Bookseller Laurent Letellier comes across an abandoned handbag
on a Parisian street, and feels impelled to return it to its owner.
The bag contains no money, phone or contact information. But
a small red notebook with handwritten thoughts and jottings
reveals a person that Laurent would very much like to meet.

Without even a name to go on, and only a few of her possessions
to help him, how is he to find one woman in a city of millions?

ISBN: 9781908313867
e-ISBN: 9781908313874